HOUSES
WINNER OF THE
HAWK MOUNTAIN AWARD

Hidden River Arts offers The Hawk Mountain Award for a book-length collection of short stories in English. The award provides both a monetary award and publication by Hidden River Publishing on its Hidden River Press imprint.

Hidden River Arts is an interdisciplinary arts organization dedicated to supporting and celebrating the unserved artists among us, particularly those outside the artistic and academic mainstream.

HOUSES

Stories by
CHARLES WYATT

HIDDEN RIVER PRESS
An imprint of Hidden River Publishing
Philadelphia, Pennsylvania

Cover and interior design by: Jana Rade

Library of Congress Number 2021953413
ISBN 978-0-9994915-7-7

HIDDEN RIVER PRESS
An imprint of Hidden River Publishing
Philadelphia, Pennsylvania

Acknowledgments

"The Blanket Chest" appeared in *The South Carolina Review*

"Sympathy for the Devil" appeared in *Concho River Review*

"The Baker Brothers" appeared in *Green Mountains Review*

"Names of the Saints" and "The Turret House" appeared in *Alaska Quarterly Review*

"Walter's House" appeared in *StorySouth*

Table of Contents

Part I (Names of the Saints)

The Blanket Chest 13

The Road to Lisdoonvarna 27

Sympathy for the Devil 39

The Baker Brothers 51

Bad Starter 63

Basswood Bend 81

Feathers 95

Names of the Saints 103

Part II (Houses)

Walter's House 111

The Station 129

Encounter 143

The Window 155

The Hockaday House 167

The Turret House 185

PART I

NAMES
OF THE
SAINTS

The Blanket Chest

We had spent a year in a small Southern city as an unmarried couple, and it hadn't been very comfortable. People looked at us in a certain way. My hair was never all that long, but I could put it in a ponytail. Anna wore long dresses – maybe it was an Amish look-alike thing. I used to get denim jackets from an Amish supply house that had snaps in the front and pockets on the inside. Think about it. The Amish don't believe in buttons.

Actually, I wanted to get married, but Anna would just say she'd always be with me so what did it matter. But it mattered to my parents, and that actually kept me on Anna's side. Long-haired hippy Amish musician artistic... what did it matter if the guy that owned The Pancake Pantry called us girls when he seated us? We weren't as cool as Richard Brautigan, but that was the picture of us I probably had in my mind's eye.

Living in a shag-floored apartment complex next to a nunnery may have compounded my guilt. Once we got out of it and moved into an old granny-stew-smelling apartment building on 17th Avenue, I felt relieved. And after I installed my plant-light fluorescents in the closet, I felt very very cool. Anna did not need to feel cool – she was cool. Anna painted large canvases (I helped her stretch them). But she spent most of her time working as a potter, throwing pots on the wheel and hand-building clay sculptures. And I had this weird orchestra job where we piled onto a bus and drove to places that didn't even have running water. Then we played classical music for the children. We might as well have set up in a pasture and played for cows.

Anna made lunches for me with hardboiled eggs and PBJ sandwiches for those runouts because the only thing I found edible in small-town middle Tennessee in those days was fried catfish. And fried catfish were the buttons in Anna's theology. Brown rice, good. Fried catfish, not good. There were two Japanese musicians in our little orchestra who could barely speak English. I called them Ha Tee one and Ha Tee two. Ha Tee is hot tea. Try to order Ha Tee in Red Boiling Springs in 1969. Then, to everyone's surprise but me, the chamber orchestra folded. Everybody got fired. The Japanese cellists went back to Japan. The oboe player went back to New York. Several of the violinists discovered they could make much more money playing recording sessions. In one studio, there was a light that went on when the tape was running that said "Now Pick." The money was good but the ambiance required some adjusting to.

What, then, became of James and Anna? The conductor hired me for another year. There would only be a handful of concerts with the larger orchestra, but he wanted me. It was only years later that I realized he liked to look at me. So it was spring – there would be a music festival in August to look forward to, but we had three long months ahead. Three long empty months.

"Let's get married."

"Why." Anna did not look at me. She was drawing a potted plant. It was a geranium. She drew it every day. She didn't look down at the drawing pad either. She looked at the geranium. It looked back at her. I looked at the geranium. It was fuzzy and had flowers I couldn't see very well because I am colorblind.

"Because we can visit my parents without my mother sighing and wringing her hands. Because she can't show us to her sister, Aunt Margaret."

"Aunt Margaret is the one who used to give you presents."

"Until Cousin Bobbie came along."

"The one who says a bird in the hand beats nothing in the bush?"

"The very one."

"And your mother is unhappy."

"She doesn't know what happy is."

"Okay." Anna stopped drawing, and I realized that the room had been filled with the sound of it, the music of those turns and swirls. Maybe it was the home-grown I was smoking in my little tinfoil pipe.

"Okay what?"

Anna gave me one of her looks. It was sad and patient and maybe a little disappointed.

"Say it," I said. "I'd like to hear you say it."

Anna began to draw again. "Okay get married." Her voice was light. She might have been asking how many hardboiled eggs I wanted for lunch.

We were married in early July in a garden in Buffalo, New York. It was a gift from The Browns, people Anna had worked for. She had been an au pair, I suppose, although we didn't use the term. There were pheasants in the garden. Bach bubbled tastefully from loudspeakers. Then we went to Niagara Falls. Anna was more interested in the kitsch shops.

I was pleased. My parents were pleased. Anna's mother sent us a fondue set. My parents welcomed us to the big white house in Fulton, and my mother showed Anna her cordial glass collection. My parents had become antique collectors. They traveled about and bought hideous plates and spoke knowledgeably about flow blue and Mary Gregory and provenance. My father refinished walnut furniture in our basement. It had always looked like a dungeon – now it smelled like one.

"What would you like for a wedding present?" my mother asked us.

"What about another fondue set?" I suggested. We had three already.

"Virginia has some new things," my father said. Virginia was my father's cousin. Virginia was an antique dealer but she did not have a shop. She sold from her house. When something was purchased, she simply replaced it from reinforcements stacked in the garage.

We visited Virginia and her husband Leonard just after supper, the traditional time for socializing in my parents' world. Virginia was quite taken with Anna and regaled her with enthusiastic baby talk of the sort that older women of a certain bent reserve for puppies and small children. Anna was a good soldier – it didn't hurt that I had warned her.

We paraded through Virginia's house, admiring various objects. (There was a hand-painted sign on the door: *Len and Gin's Antiques n' Stuff*. (That was my first lifetime *n' Stuff* sighting.) Early on, Leonard, a very tall and taciturn man, took his huge feet to the garage where he probably cobbled and stirred, and perhaps forged. In our alligator, my father followed Virginia, my mother followed my father, Anna followed my mother and I milled about, having lost my electric charge, in very much the same manner I had in the shops in Niagara Falls.

I liked the old furniture, and Anna seemed to admire the teapots and glass objects. Many things were charming. I admired something that looked like a kerosene lamp with a reflector attached. I learned that it was a caboose lantern and that it had been attached to a train in its former life. Now it could be attached to a wall and it would burn something called lamp oil that would smell nicer than kerosene but probably would not as effectively repel chiggers if rubbed on one's ankles. The lamp was given to us. It was an *old thing* rather than an antique. What else would we like? I had swung at the piñata and now it was leaking. I could tell my mother was pleased.

Virginia suggested we go to the garage. Apparently it is possible for the inside of a structure to be larger than the outside. We toiled about and viewed chairs stacked upon chairs and the backsides of roll-top desks. I sat down, exhausted.

"James, what are you sitting on?" Anna exclaimed.

I righted myself and Leonard removed a large stack of newspapers obscuring a very large object, which might have been Queequeg's coffin had it not been perfectly rectangular. I knew it was not walnut, and that my parents only showed interest in walnut furniture. It was a box with a lid and a little molding around the bottom. Nothing could have been plainer. Or larger.

"It's an old pine blanket chest, dearie," Virginia said, dismissively.

"It's beautiful," Anna said.

"Then you must have it," said Virginia.

I raised the lid and saw there were, in fact, old blankets inside it. It did not smell of cedar or pine – it smelled of old blankets. There was a primitive sliding rack that could be moved from side to side. There was room inside for at least two consenting adults.

"How would you ever move it anywhere?" my mother asked. My mother was good at foreseeing difficulties.

* * *

The blanket chest fit nicely into the corner of a U Haul trailer. My mother threw in a maple table and a few chairs. Even an old upholstered easy chair that had been moved upstairs to make room for the new uncomfortable antique walnut furniture. There was a big sign on the trailer that posted a warning of 45 mph speed limit. We never got close to it. My Rambler American was not much for towing.

Back in Nashville, the chest had to be moved up two flights of stairs, but we were young and strong, and had not seen many Laurel and Hardy episodes. Then it rested beneath a window, suddenly becoming the most important object in our living room.

"What do you want to keep in it?" I asked Anna. The lid was heavy and much scratched. Virginia had described it as distressed.

The only blankets we had were on the bed. Our books were proudly displayed on cinder-block bookcases.

"Nothing."

Anna put a ceramic sculpture on it. It was raku fired and looked like an enormous milkweed pod, just getting ready to burst open. Then I understood. It was not a chest. It was a display stand. The milkweed pod sculpture looked splendid on the distressed pine. The chest had been stained brown. Most of the rest of our furniture was painted flat black. Brown was a cheerful contrast.

It was about this time that I started making bamboo flutes. With various improvised tools I could hollow out a length of fishing-pole sized bamboo and drill finger holes with a dull drill bit. I had been inspired by recordings of Indian music. I wanted to make a really big flute, but I couldn't fine large bore bamboo. So I practiced making small flutes that were about a foot long. I had read Theobald Boehm's *The Flute and Flute Playing*, but I decided against a scientific approach to the project. I held a blank piece of cane as if it were a finished flute and marked the places where my fingers touched. After I drilled the holes and plugged the top end, I had a little flute, that, after a little pocket knife tuning, produced a scale at least the equal of a plastic song flute. By sliding my fingers and changing the angle of blowing, I could bend the sound. The result might have seemed to some listeners very like the sound of an Indian flute. To others, it might have recalled the early stages of a cat fight. I made at least a dozen of the little flutes, and Anna began to take an interest in them.

After I showed her how to get a sound, she needed no further encouragement. She used the flutes for meditation, I think. She played little bird calls or animal sounds, and even to my conservatory-trained ears, those sounds were interesting. Sometimes I played with her, producing what I felt were similar sounds, and while she didn't discourage me, I came to understand that she was playing for some other reason.

She was playing for the blanket chest. She always sat down in front of it before she began to play, and then for as long as a half an hour at a stretch she would play her little flute, making what I came to think of as shapes and gestures of sound. It was like listening to a language I did not understand or even to voices speaking in another room, too distant for the meaning to fall into place.

Anna decorated her little flutes with a wood-burning tool, and even the decorations seemed to lurk just on the far side of meaning. And when she was done, she put the little flutes inside the blanket chest, first carefully removing the milkweed pod sculpture, and then replacing it. It had become a ritual, some kind of tea ceremony.

Anna was always a quiet person and she seemed particularly dreamy and distracted after her music. I had a studio at the local college, and I began doing my regular practicing there. After a few weeks, our apartment heard only the bamboo flutes which, I began to suspect, Anna played in a fixed rotation.

I sat at my desk in the opposite end of the room, listening. I wasn't excluded, but it wasn't something we talked about.

"Why do you play the little flutes in front of the blanket chest?" was simply not a question I could ask her. I understood I had to come to an understanding on my own. So I sat and listened, imagining that my Anna was playing a musical composition. But there was no structure there. I could go for a walk around the block and hear as much structure from the robins and mourning doves and blue jays and starlings. I did. But when I returned, Anna would still be whittling little shavings of sound. I sat at my desk. In the kitchen, the refrigerator motor cut out. The room immediately seemed larger. Anna took no notice.

There was a yellow legal pad on the desk. I used it to jot down ideas for poems and stories. Sometimes weeks would go by between orchestra rehearsals. There was a great deal of time to fill. Anna and I would go to the college in the afternoon, she to her classes and her work, I to practice and to see a few students. But our mornings were for this business of her playing and me listening.

It was too serious an enterprise to be entertaining. But it was not frustrating. I fully expected to understand what she was doing, what I was doing, eventually. I supposed it had something to do with patience. Patience. It *had* to do with patience.

While she played, I found myself jotting down the lines of a poem. It was a poem about a tree. One day it was a tree, another day it was a vine, another day moss. The tree was growing. The vine was growing. Ditto the moss. The poem, which I soon realized was supposed to be a long poem, a very long poem – the poem was growing. Perhaps I was translating Anna's music.

The poem is gone now, lost to me, lost to Anna. Lost to the world, I should say if I stay close to the character I was then, earnest, believer in magic, in secrets. I can remember its first line: "There is the tree." *There is the tree.* Not "Look out, there's a tree at the door!" Not "It's trying to get in!" Not a single exclamation mark. My poem was going to be long and it was going to be – let's not say bad – let's not say useless – let's say inapplicable. So Anna played, day after day, her little flutes in front of the blanket chest. And James worked on the poem. One morning Anna put down her flute and sat in quiet for a moment. Then she began the ceremony of removing the milkweed pod raku sculpture and restoring the flutes. The sculpture seemed to me to be swelling – its petals were opening – I knew it was the light, or maybe the dope. Now the little flutes were rolled up in colorful pieces of cloth. Without thinking, I rose and took my sheaves of vegetable poetry and placed them in the open chest. Anna looked at me the way a border collie looks at a sheep. Then she smiled.

"Yes," she said, and she closed the chest.

In August we drove to Wisconsin where I played in a music festival with rehearsals every day and frequent concerts. We had a cabin in the woods with no near neighbors. Anna had brought one of her flutes and she played it out of doors most mornings. I had to rise early to get a page of my long poem before the morning rehearsal.

We took long walks together. We watched sunsets over the water. There was a little store where we bought ice cream cones. The music-making was exciting but also exhausting. I took naps between rehearsals. Anna puttered, as she called it.

A single day seemed endless but the aggregate of the three weeks rushed by breathlessly.

On the last night, after the last concert, we were startled awake by a sharp cracking sound inside the cabin. Could it have been a shot? I turned on the bedside lamp.

"Something bad," said Anna.

I looked around the other rooms. No bear. No raccoon or other intruder. Then on my way back into the bedroom, I saw it. Anna's flute hung from a nail in the cedar-paneled wall. I had made a lanyard for it with a leather bootlace. The flute had split from one end to the other. The resultant crack was not so much a crack as an abyss.

I brought it into the bedroom and handed it to her.

"I can make another when we get home."

Anna shook her head.

"It's just a flute. It's not like…"

Why did I feel responsible? I hadn't done anything wrong. Well, I had done plenty of things wrong, but this wasn't it.

The next morning we finished packing the car and began the drive home. Green Bay, Milwaukee, Chicago. All those miles of unmoving flat fields with tiny farm houses in the distance. The hot wind buffeting our mutual silence. The car had a radio but we didn't play it. Indianapolis. We plunged south. Kentucky. It had been dark for hours. Anna slept and I drove on.

When we reached our apartment house, I didn't want to wake her. In the car, I slept, too.

I woke with a very stiff neck to bright sunlight. A dozen robins were scavenging the lawn between me and our building. Anna was gone. I unfolded myself and, taking only my flute, climbed the stairs. The creaking seemed to be coming from me. Familiar old place. Familiar but mysterious cooking behind doors. Our door was slightly ajar.

Anna was sitting in the middle of the floor. The blanket chest was open, its lid resting against the wall behind it. In front, in the place where Anna usually sat to play her bamboo flutes, lay the scattered shards of the raku sculpture – then I noticed other broken pots. The room was a battlefield.

"Something bad," I said, remembering. Then, "Was the door open?" And when Anna didn't answer, "Was the door unlocked? Anna." I was becoming angry. I spoke harshly.

"The door was locked," she finally said.

I saw she had been crying quietly. I got down on the floor and tried to embrace her but she shook me off. More creaking of knees. I got a broom and swept the broken pottery into piles. Nothing seemed repairable but I didn't trust myself to throw anything away. Anna took herself to the bedroom finally and lay down.

I unpacked our things. All that stair-climbing was good for me. I was limber again. No longer angry at myself. I hadn't done anything wrong. Pots will break.

Anna seemed restored. She made us tea. What had happened? Could it have been vandalism? The door had really been locked. The chest had been closed. It was Anna herself who had opened it. Could there have been an earthquake? The old building seemed to shake when a truck went by or in a high wind. Large tree limbs scraped the windows when it stormed. The tree outside our window was full of robins. They were flocking. We had never seen the like. I resolved to ask the neighbors.

We went to the Pancake Pantry at my insistence. I ate pancakes and sweet syrup and butter. Anna ate, too. The syrup was thick and slow. It seemed healing to us.

"The flutes are cracked, too," Anna said. "All of them."

"I'm sorry." I knew I shouldn't say I could make more of them. I knew I would. That I would make large ones and small ones and play them myself. That I would keep them in the chest, and then when there were too many, stand them in corners in baskets.

I didn't know it would take me another year to finish the poem, and that I would type its pages and keep it in the chest. One day, years later, long after Anna and I had parted ways, I would open the lid, and, wearing gloves because of the dust, fill a large heavy-duty shopping bag with the many copies of the poem I had made, not even keeping one to read in moments like this.

That evening a waitress asked us if we would like anything else. I paid the bill and we walked home together, holding hands. The next morning the robins gathered in flocks in the trees and were restless for hours before flying away for good. We never saw them again.

The Road to Lisdoonvarna

ames was walking down the dog food isle of the IGA when a large man blocked his passage and stared at him in seeming amazement. There was no way to get around him because his shopping cart was at right angles to the aisle. The man had thin red hair and wore a very large Hawaiian shirt. He seemed familiar...

"Mickey. Is that you?"

The man lunged at James and hugged him so hard two cans of dog food fell out of his hand basket and rolled down the aisle toward a charcoal briquette display.

"James, James. I am me. Always have been. Where have you been – I heard you moved to Ohio."

While James explained that he only taught in Ohio, that

he still lived in Nashville, Mickey rearranged his cart to allow the passage of shoppers, and fastidiously retrieved the dog food cans. He was agile for a large man, and he seemed to have aged gracefully, retired now from the symphony at least 15 years. James had lost touch with him, had even heard one report that he was dead.

"What are you doing now?" James asked as he moved out of the way of a woman groping in the Fancy Feast cans.

"There are no Seafood Feasts, Madame. I have already looked. But the ground manatee is delicious." The woman looked at Mickey with his bright orange and purple shirt and glowing smile, snatched a few cans and hurried away.

"Not a damn thing. I am retired. I am a freelance greeter, helping out the lost shoppers of the world, like that poor woman. I considered saying something indecent to her, but I have changed. I am a very much changed man, reformed in fact."

"Right," said James. "Well, it's been great to see you."

"In fact, I lied about doing nothing. I have taken up fishing. I fish all the time."

"I'd love to go with you sometime," James said over his shoulder as he walked away from the knot of stalled shoppers that Mickey and his cart had managed to beaver dam in the aisle. James hated yakking women who tied up traffic in the supermarket – now he was doing it himself.

"Today," Mickey yelled. Several people turned their carts around and fled. Mickey's face was red and he was waving his hands over his head although James had only made about ten feet of his escape. James halted as if ordered. Mickey looked like he was having a fit.

"Today," he said again in an almost normal voice. "Let's go fishing today. I was planning to go this afternoon. I'll have you home in time for supper. "Today. Today." He was doing an ET voice. Yes, this was Mickey.

"Well, I've got a concert this evening. It's not a concert concert but the Celtic group I play with has got a gig in a new pub.

"Great, I'll come. I'm Irish. I dream in Gaelic. You got nothing else to do but play music tonight?" More shoppers elbowing by. "You still live in the same place?"

James had a brief impulse to run. Mickey had been his roommate on tour. They had drunk a lot of Jack Daniels together. *Too much time is passing. Think of something. Too late.*

"I'll come by your house in an hour. Okay – an hour and a half. I've got plenty of tackle, you don't have to bring a thing. Just feed the dogs and cats – home by supper. We'll catch a manatee or two. You know those things are anatomically kind of like sheep, but ugly. All sheep are pretty, Montana blonds. You know what Proust said – 'Leave the pretty women to the men without imagination' – no not the Proust you're thinking about – my neighbor, Benny Proust."

Mickey wandered off, still talking, leaving James with his basket and two dented cans of Alpo.

"You're going fishing?" James' wife Mary put down the book she was reading. "Didn't you say you'd never get in a car with Mickey Molloy again?"

"Oh that. Well, he missed the deer. It was a pretty nifty piece of driving, actually. And that was back in the day. He's probably a grownup now."

"I'll bet. We're going to try to start the first set at 8:30. You'd better drive by yourself. I can set up the sound with Matt."

"You don't mind?"

"Just don't wear yourself out. That guy's crazy."

"We had good times."

"So did Bonny and Clyde, Thelma and Louise."

"We're going fishing."

"So you say."

It was a johnboat, not a bass boat – Mickey made the distinction seem important – as far as James could tell, it was a boat on a trailer you backed down a ramp and which miraculously floated. And no, it did not have a john.

"It is safest to pee over the stern," Mickey said, but avoid the outboard motor – we are not carrying oars. James allowed he would hold his water but then Mickey showed him that the cooler was not for fish.

"We will catch and release and keep the beer cold. Now I hope you can appreciate the technology. This is a fish finder and it shows them in Technicolor."

There was a colorful screen which might have belonged to a video game. James could not see it well because he was hunched over to avoid the spray from waves breaking in a noisy washboard effect.

"Do you have to go this fast? You're loosening my fillings."

"Just a minute more. Aha, here it is." Mickey cut the motor and let out an anchor on a long line. "Creek bed."

James looked around. Mickey had parked the boat in what seemed to be the middle of the lake, a featureless expanse of rather choppy water. It was a July afternoon, but the sky had become overcast and there was a strong breeze.

"What creek bed?"

"Down there, my lad. Think of it as the seafood aisle. I want you to take this rig and let it fall to the bottom." Mickey gave James a spinning rod and reel with a huge weight on the end and a loathsome plastic lizard or salamander dangling above it, very much the same color as Mickey's shirt. "The bass will ingest it gently. You'll have to develop a subtle sense of touch."

James made a short cast and allowed his rig to plummet down to the sunken creekbed. "What if that tungsten spark plug lands on the fish and stuns it? Will it float to the surface?"

"No. It will slink away and gather up its fellows in a fish army, and they will come and sing to us bawdy fish songs, bass ballades, sunfish serenades. Here, have a beer."

James tried to imagine his lizard darting and falling, darting and falling, but all he could picture was a yo-yo.

"Can the bass see these things?"

"They see, they hear, they smell. What's time to a bass?"

"What's time?"

"They don't philosophize – they're not much on abstract concepts."

"Got any worms?"

"Just keep jigging and have another beer."

Mickey caught several large bass. He would begin to hum under his breath, then yank back on his rod to set the hook. The bass was hauled up to the surface where it splashed and roiled in an entertaining way, then it was released. James began to notice the tune Mickey was humming.

"What is that you're humming?"

"Oh, an old tune my mother used to sing."

"I know that tune – it's no lullaby."

"Can you play it then? It's a fiddle tune. The bass remind me of it when they dance."

"Funny thing – when I go fishing I seldom bring fiddle or flute."

"Funny thing, just look in this box. You open it my lad, because I've got fish on my hands and I smell like pussy."

James put his rod down. The lizard could take a coffee break. The box which Mickey took from under his seat was an old instrument case and when James opened it, he found a wood flute.

"What are you doing with an old flute?"

"I found it in a pawn shop and bought it for fifty bucks."

"And you keep it in your bass boat."

"Johnboat, Jimmy. I thought of you and tossed it in. Turns out I am not much of a fluter. Play us a tune, me and the fishes."

James put the flute together and tried it. It had several keys but they weren't necessary for "The Road to Lisdoonvarna."

"That's it. That's my tune. Play us another. Can you do 'Brown Ale?'"

It was not a bad little flute. James left off lizard jiggling and played jigs instead. Mickey brought bass from the creek bed to tours of the surface which was getting rather choppy. James put the flute away.

"Mickey, let's go home. I've got to play tonight."

"Yes, yes, we'll get you home, and you can take that little flute if you like – but I want to show you something first. It's my UFO. Well forget I said that, then. I wouldn't think you'd give an old friend such an exasperated look. Let's just say I want to show you something interesting, and then we'll head on home. Reel in your critter. Really, I could have sworn you'd catch something with that, but I appreciate the music. You know I don't play anymore. I sold my horns. Don't miss that part of it a bit. I'll bet you don't either, playing in little jam bands with harps and fiddles. You should learn the pipes – now there's music to wake the dead."

Mickey stowed the tackle, and after several unsettling attempts, got the outboard started.

James wondered if fishing boats ever broke up from the pelting washboard effect of the chop. He pushed the little flute box further under his seat. It once had a leather veneer, but most of that had worn off, leaving bare wood. The flute had had a long life but now was in much better shape than its ancient case.

Mickey rounded a point and brought the boat into calmer water. The shoreline was a steep bluff, quarry-like. They scooted along the bluff until they rounded another point and James could see the consternation on Mickey's face. As Mickey throttled down the outboard, James turned and saw another fishing party, apparently having discovered Mickey's spot. Mickey cut the motor.

"Crappie fishing," Mickey said to James. Then to the boat, "Catching any?" Then to James, "They still-fish with minnows. The crappie school around the UFO. I wish I'd never told them."

"Just got here," someone called from the boat, a hearty looking woman who might be in her sixties. The other angler made a short cast, a kind of two-handed heave, necessitated by the distance between the bobber and the weighted minnow. Another woman of indeterminate age, dressed in camouflage.

"Have you heard about the weather?" Mickey called. "Bad storm coming up. Lightning and hail. Waterspouts. Cats and dogs."

"Not in this county," the woman in camouflage returned.

"That's my UFO down there." They had drifted so close that Mickey no longer had to raise his voice."

"Is that Mickey Molloy?" the first woman said.

"And is that Margaret Sheenan?" Mickey said, now affecting an Irish lilt.

"Who's your friend?"

"Oh this is Jimmy, my old buddy from orchestra days. I brought him to see my UFO."

"Well can you show him without drifting over our fishing? We were here first, after all."

"Margaret, there's plenty of those bony little critters for all of us, and besides, we're done fishing for the day. Put down that anchor Jimmy."

James let down the anchor and nearly all the rope paid out before it struck bottom.

"Near sixty foot right next to the bluff. Then it falls off more. Now, come look at my fish finder."

James made his way to the console and made more of an effort to see what was on the screen. A big 75 rode the top of the screen. "Seventy-five feet deep?"

"You got it."

And the split screen appeared to show a horizontal and a vertical view but it looked more like a weather map than a lake bottom. James couldn't see anything that looked like individual fish or even groups of fish. But on the bottom there was an object, roughly spherical in the vertical view.

"What is that? That thing on the bottom. Is it some kind of structure? Somebody's house?"

"There's an old road down there, and that's the police station. And there are the little people riding their bicycles back and forth." Mickey pointed to orange blobs on the screen.

"Those are fish?"

"Fish or bicycles, take your pick."

"Okay. What is it? Really."

"Tell him the story you told me," Margaret said, reeling in a silvery speckled fish about the size of an outstretched hand.

"Last summer I was fishing over there – that point extends a long way and the bass gather on it like sheep on a hillside. And it was late. Whippoorwills had started up. Then I saw this thing flying along the face of the bluff. It was orange and glowing – just like a big old firefly."

"And it sat down on the water and laid an egg," Margaret said, "and then it floated back up over the bluffs and buzzed back to Jupiter. And now we've got the best Crappie school in the lake. And only me and Mickey know about it."

"I don't know about it," the other woman said, "because if I did, I'd be as crazy as they are."

James looked at the fish finder again. There was something on the bottom. But these lakes had covered farms and even villages. Maybe it was a silo.

"Mickey, I've got a gig tonight. You promised you would get me home. I'm pleased to have met you Margaret, and…"

"Joan," the camouflage woman said. "The sane one."

"James, James, you don't believe me, do you."

"I believe you've found a great fishing spot," James said, watching Joan pull in another pan-sized fish.

"Do one more thing, then," Mickey said. "Take out that flute and play us a tune. Play "The Road to Lisdoonvarna."

"And you'll take me home then?"

"Boat or bicycle, you can make the call."

James took the little flute out of its case, noticing for the first time that someone had replaced the velvet lining. It was getting dark and the red velvet seemed to glow. James played the tune twice and then threw in "Haste to the Wedding."

"There. Two jigs for the price of one. I'll take the boat ride, Mickey."

"Now James, just give it a minute. Don't look at the fish finder. Look over the side. Look carefully."

The water was very clear. James had seen the bass Mickey caught darting about at least six feet under the water, maybe even more. But how do you know what you are looking at when there's nothing to see?

"What am I looking for?" James asked.

"There. That's what you're looking for."

And James saw something. A flashing light. For a moment, and then it was gone.

"We'll be taking our leave, ladies." Mickey started the outboard motor on the first attempt and then raised his eyebrows in James' direction.

"If you would be so kind as to pull in the anchor."

James laid the flute on its case which rested on the seat next to him and began to pull up the anchor rope. Somehow, the old flute case came apart and when James tried to grab the flute, the case lid levered the flute up and over the edge of the johnboat where it sank like a rock.

"I've heard that blackwood will sink in water. Never tested it before," Mickey said quietly.

"Oh damn." James could imagine the flute tumbling down in the dark water. "I'm sorry."

"Good-bye." Margaret and her sane friend Joan waved over the curve of their wake as they pulled away. And the johnboat rocked as the wake banged against it, twice, three times. And then, the outboard motor quit. The silence was like a slap in the face. Margaret and Joan were already too distant to hail. Mickey tried a few more pulls on the starter rope. Then he looked at James and shrugged.

"What was that light?" James asked.

"Beats me." Mickey said. Another wake gently rocked the johnboat and a whippoorwill called from the top of the bluff. It was a very peaceful evening.

James could see Mary and Matt setting up. Matt refused to use a tuner so after Mary had tuned the harp methodically up and down, Matt would tune his guitar and then the cittern string by string, taking as long as it took to tune the harp. They would start without him. Somebody would probably sit in after a while.

"Are we out of gas?" James asked.

"I've got a paddle," Mickey said. "We can take turns. We'll be at the ramp in a few hours with any luck... But now, would you look at that."

A light was flashing again from beneath them. Maybe it was a reflection – but the sky was dark. It was a small light – or a distant light.

"Jimmy, do you see?"

"Of course, I see."

"No. Listen, I mean."

There was nothing. Not even a whippoorwill. Just the quiet lapping of waves against the bluff.

"Oh. You don't think..."

Mickey began to whistle, exactly in time to the flashing light. A slow jig. The one James had just played.

James took the paddle after the light stopped flashing. Mickey had left off whistling, too, but James could still hear the tune in his head.

"There *is* a road down there," Mickey said.

"Could you rig that lizard thing for me?" James asked. "We might as well fish a little longer."

"But we might catch something."

James nodded his head. "Yes, we just might."

Sympathy for the Devil

Winters in Ohio are tedious. They are tedious most everywhere, I suppose. But I am thinking of a time, only a few years ago, it seems, when winters were more dedicated, more relentless, when the ice stayed in place for several months and you had to wax the dog's feet before a walk and wash them afterward to get rid of the ice. Ice. Ice was in the air and on the streets and sidewalks and hanging from the eves of my little house. And it hung from the deadfall trees on the Middleton College hillside. The colors of my world were black and white and gray. And by the end of March, I didn't think I was going to make it to the end of the term. My poodle, Lucy, was crabby and didn't want to go for her constitutional walks. I had to drag her out the door. My neighbor across the street, Doris, had a dog, too – an elderly, overweight bulldog named Daisy, and we commiserated – we were dog owners with cranky, ungrateful dogs who chewed and did inside the things dogs should do outside. Doris was overweight like Daisy, but Doris still had vim. She waved and encouraged me as I dragged Lucy like a sledge out into the wilderness each morning, slogging in the new snow.

"Good work, Professor. You're a good daddy," she would call as I dragged the nearly full-grown puppy by her cottage.

"This is how they train for the Iditarod." I laughed and urged the puppy on. I could see Daisy the bulldog squatting only two feet from her front door. Lucy could not be persuaded to do her business within the radius of a city block. I trudged and dragged, filled with visions of Jack London, of wolves and dogs, and of the many ways a person could freeze to death. I hadn't brought matches with me. There would be no fire lighting fiascos.

I had elected to head up the college hill. Sometimes Lucy would become inspired closer to home, I theorized, if we climbed uphill. And sure enough, she became suddenly enlivened and dashed up the steep hillside, nearly wrenching the lead out of my hand, knocking the snow off a large clump of dead weeds which turned out to be loaded with clumps of cockleburs. Then she theatrically rolled away, pawing at the deeply entangled burs. Two hundred yards from my house, in four inches of snow, I was pulling burs off my poodle, or pulling my poodle off a quantity of burs so large, they had the commanding presence. And most of the burs I got off the dog ended up stuck on my own clothing.

"Well done, Professor," Doris waved to me again as we staggered back down the hill. Daisy was in the same place, still straining unsuccessfully. We both looked at Daisy. Lucy wagged her tail, which still sported several burs. Doris shrugged. Doris lived alone and sometimes brought me jars of what she described as chicken soup. After trying the first offering, I flushed them routinely, but I always accepted them with gratitude. That Doris lived a lonely life I was certain. If I were to put us together in a story, our small talk about dogs and squirrels and recipes for chicken soup would dwindle into weighty silence. And I could scarcely hold up the burden of the individual silence in my real life. Stay out of that story then, I told myself.

But that day, with the ice-encrusted burs swinging in Lucy's tail as she appreciated Daisy's Sisyphean efforts from afar, Doris was loquacious.

"It's hard to believe spring will be here soon. Crocus and daffodils. And the fish will be jumping in Middleton pond."

I waved, unwilling to further this renga of small talk into another season, impossible concept to comprehend.

Daffodils and jumping fish. What was she thinking about? I filled a saucepan with warm water and went to work removing the ice from the dog's feet. We were friends again. She tenderly licked my hand as I washed and dried: dogleg left, dogleg right. Now for the scissors and the burs.

My office neighbor, Dennis Kessler, was waiting for me when I slogged in with books and briefcase.

"Good morning, Tommy O," he said cheerfully. "Farmer's Almanac predicts an early spring. Don't look so glum. By the way, you've been selected to read student stories for the yearbook contest." He handed me a huge bundle of file folders. "It was a close contest between you and E. L. Doctorow, but you won. We knew you would."

It was a weighty stack. I could tell what I had in store. My left brain can read the past and the future. Several cells packed their bags and deserted. Enough is enough, they cried. My right brain knows only the present. The present is gray and is covered with ice.

"Dennis, I have been told there are seasons. I seem to remember seasons." I hefted the student stories like a butcher appraising a flounder. "But I don't believe in seasons – I have been told there are good stories..."

"Now don't say it. There is a Santa Claus. What's the matter, Tommy O?"

"I want to go fishing. I want to throw out a minnow or a worm and watch a damsel fly light on my bobber. I want to step in muskrat holes and sprain my ankle the way I did when I was a kid. Say, what is Middleton Pond?"

"Middleton Pond? It's on college property. Behind the guest house. I haven't been there in years, but that's where you should go fishing. It's completely restricted to the public. Only faculty can go there – all you have to do is go to the Provost's office and fill out a dozen forms. If you start now, you'll be legal when the weather breaks."

"You want to go?"

"No. I don't like fish. I don't like to get wet. I don't like the groundskeeper. When the snow melts, I'll play golf – one silly recreation is as good as the next. I enjoy looking for golf balls – it's very much like fishing, now that I think about it."

A few weeks passed and, to my amazement, the weather broke. I had followed Dennis's directions and gotten a permission sheet from the Provost's office which allowed me on the grounds of Middleton House and, specifically, the south forty, where could be found, according to everyone I talked to, Middleton Pond.

It was Saturday and Lucy had managed to find the weed with the cockleburs and prove to me that burs can replenish themselves even in the dead of winter. All the snow had melted except for a few lonely strips and ragged patches that never saw the sun. I had gathered up my fishing tackle and my nearly bur-less poodle, and I was going fishing.

Lucy did not want to get in the car, but finally agreed to accompany me if she could bring along a hideous and slimy chew bone.

The guest house was only a few miles from the college hill campus, situated in rolling pasture land. We parked in an empty lot – the house seemed deserted – and walked for a quarter of a mile, following the map I had been provided. Freed from her leash, Lucy found more burs – tiny ones and large ones. We were both delighted. Finally, we came upon the pond. Lake size it was. There's some confusion in my mind about labeling lakes and ponds. Ponds should be small. But this was a Walden Pond, a stately spread – like the lake at Bly, that slough in *The Turn of the Screw* which also gets called a pond, I think. No apparitions apparent. Lucy and I would have the place to ourselves. I proceeded to attach a variety of artificial lures and cast them out, over and into the green water, while Lucy undertook to drink it all. This can only be done by wading forth, stirring up the bottom, and then bounding to dry land with the intention of shaking as much water on the fisherman as possible. The water was cold. The air was cold. The fisherman and the dog were foolish. The dog bounded about, chasing Quint and Miss Jessel, for all I could tell. I caught a few small and foolish fish with a lure I knew in my youth as a Pico Perch, but which now had some other name: Dreadful Drizzler or Boiling Bream. It vibrated like Nellie

Melba if you pulled it fast enough through the water and fish bit it out of consternation. If the hooks hadn't all been in their mouths, I would have assumed I had snagged them as they floated about in a frozen stupor.

After a while, Lucy became less frenzied and sat near me while I cast out and reeled in, giving the impression that we were fisherman and dog, rather than what it was we actually were: jaded academic and familiar.

I decided to make a circuit of the pond. Perhaps we would stumble on Thoreau's cabin and he would pour us tea, or show us that trick of pocketing crickets frozen in ice and then having them hop about after the thaw. There were patches of delicate ice where the water was shallow. I thought I saw small frogs but my eyes have reached the stage where I nearly always see small frogs, and most of them indoors. There were stretches of shoreline where the dense brush and small trees had woven down to the water's edge and presented an impenetrable barrier. These we circled around and out-flanked. When we were on the far side of the pond, one large copse caused us to make an excessive detour which involved crossing a deep gully, stepping on rocks, or wading in mud, depending upon personal preference, or in some cases, personal misfortunate. We climbed up the other side of the gully and Lucy alerted me with her warning bark, a kind of *sotto voce* "whuff," a sound both discreet and alarming.

Between us and the lake shore (the body of water had suddenly become more imposing) stood a man in a posture of authority, legs spread and one hand holding an impressive walking stick. The sun was behind him so I couldn't make out his features, but he seemed to be garbed in the standard Orvis outdoorsman regalia.

The groundskeeper? Another eccentric faculty fisherman? No. He had no gear besides that staff. An escapee from Henry James? Lucy whined, a call for action. We had been standing and staring at each other long enough for my feet to have begun sliding back down the side of the gulley. I hopped clear in what I hoped was both a sprightly and agile motion. Lucy actually growled.

"Hello," I said.

From Quint, or let's call him Mickey, nothing. I noticed now he was bearded.

"Are you the groundskeeper? I checked at the guest house but nobody seemed to be at home."

"Let's see your pass," said the shadowy fellow, beginning now to approach us. His walking stick was carved and intricate, but eyes that tend to make up small frogs may be excused if they imagine anything seeming to writhe.

I had the pass in my shirt pocket and produced it with no further comment except for a few paternal steadying admonitions directed at Lucy, who was leaning on me so hard, I might have benefited from a staff myself.

To better examine my pass, Quint thrust the staff in the soft earth and there it stood on its own, the carvings of what I could now see were entwined serpents seeming to squirm and wiggle. Hawthorne would have said a trick of the light. I blinked and the staff reset. Lucy growled again. Quint handed me my pass.

"Enjoy your fishing then, Professor Walker," he said. "You're going to have to bathe your dog."

"You have the advantage," I said. "I don't know your name."

"Oh my name is Bill. I'm not the caretaker but I help out some days. This is the farm, you know, of the Middletons who founded the college. Most of them are buried in the little cemetery at the top of the campus, but one, Samuel, is buried here. There's a small graveyard here on the farm and I tend it. It's just behind the guest house."

"It's good to know you, Bill."

"Probably not. I'm also the devil."

On hearing this announcement, I looked Bill over more carefully. He wasn't a good candidate for Lucifer, I decided. He was a short man – this had been disguised from me at first because I was viewing him from the gulley. He wore a little pork pie fishing hat and his eyes, which might have been smoldering and commanding, were small and deep set. He looked for all the world like a blind man.

"You're the devil," I repeated, expecting, I suppose for him to correct me with I'm the devil of a groundskeeper or I make the best deviled eggs in the county.

Lucy leaned against me again, almost upsetting my balance. I believe she wanted to bring me to my senses.

"Yes, I'm the devil. And they don't pay me enough." Bill pulled his staff from the ground, producing a rather festive pop. The dog was astounded, and if I had not restrained her would have pounced on the hole in the mud.

"Well, that's a complaint most of us have," I said, wondering how I was ever going to get rid of crazy Bill.

"You don't believe I'm the devil."

"I'll have to admit I'm dubious. But I really don't want to encourage you to do anything devilish. I suppose I'd be pleased if you could do something magical – three wishes, for instance. Or you could just vanish."

"I'll turn your dog into a fish."

I can talk a traffic cop into changing a ticket for running a red light into a warning, but I can't get out of a conversation with Bill the devil without pissing him off.

"I'd much rather catch my own fish. That's why I'm here. That's why I have that pass I showed you. Why don't we just leave it at that? Come on Lucy." But there at my feet, still leaning against me, was a huge carp. It flopped once and then lay in the weeds, its mouth blowing bubbles or making O's, its tail flexing slightly.

I looked up and Bill was gone. I was alone in the Middleton farm pasture with a carp. It occurred to me that I should put Lucy the carp back in the lake. Back in the lake? I picked up the fish with both hands and held it against my chest cradled in my elbows. It was wet and slimy, but it did not struggle. It was also extremely heavy.

What else to do? I struggled with my cursed poodle to the muddy edge of the lake and tossed it in. There was a huge writhing splash – nearly as much activity as Charlton Heston created when he parted the Red Sea – and then, out of the water struggled, in a grand dog paddle, poodle Lucy, joyously shaking water to all points of the compass and managing through persistent jumping, to get most of it on me.

For one wet dog restored I was hugely grateful. Toward one missing groundskeeper named Bill aka The Devil, I was alert. Concerning my own sanity, I was not especially sanguine. If only I had snapped a cell phone portrait of Lucy's temporary incarnation. But who reminds themselves to be prepared for such things? Now I was a member of the poodle-carp-poodle society and proud I had no documentation.

I fished for another hour before a cold front came with furious winds which brought whitecaps to every third or fourth wave. At the point where we began our morning of fishing and conversations with strangers I saw a large snapping turtle swimming lazily along the shore and I swiped at it with my red tip, expecting some lively turtle swimming, perhaps. Instead, the thing snagged onto my lure, and began to pull out the light weight monofilament line prodigiously. I cut the line with my pocketknife, unwilling to pull another large object out of Middleton pond. Ovid would take a serious interest in Middleton pond.

I know there is still a large turtle trailing 30 yards of nylon line, probably entangling rainbow trout and baby bunnies, but I had no other choice.

Lucy and I shivered and hopped through the burs, thorns and wild rose vines until we got to my car which still had a wet dog mark on the passenger side of the front seat. The guest house was dark – no cars save mine were in the lot – but I thought I saw the blinds at a window facing us twitch.

On our way home, it began to snow. I had to slow down – a blizzard.

After drying the dog and wrapping the fisherman around some good brown corn whiskey, I realized it was time for Lucy's constitutional.

Of course, Doris and Daisy were laboring in her now snowy postage stamp of a front yard.

"Hello Professor. It's wonderful weather we're having," Doris said as Daisy strained and crab-walked about, probably suffering terminal aging bulldog embarrassment. "Did you go fishing before the blizzard hit?"

"Yes, but then we met the devil and Lucy was turned into a carp."

That shut Doris up. She looked at me sadly. I was pulling the leg of a kind neighbor, one who had brought me soup. I felt bad. First the devil, then the turtle, and now this.

"It was only temporary," I said. "I probably imagined it." I could tell Doris was relieved. Lucy pulled me on, choosing the path up the hill. I had never noticed that slightly undulating motion in her gait before.

The Baker Brothers

James often began his Saturdays by wandering in the fallow cornfield behind his house. Farther on, he would cross the white tailings of an abandoned clay mine where he might find a scattering of puddles, tinted an odd blue by the minerals in the clay, populated by an occasional frog. Leopard frogs principally, but also a wandering green frog, sometimes spring peepers, toads. James was ten-years-old, a solitary and thoughtful child. On this particular day there was a splash and he watched the little creature bury itself in the clay at the bottom of the two inches of ridiculously clear water. He reached down and closed his fingers over the squirming mix of cold mud and slick frog. It was a leopard frog, two stripes down its back and spotted. When it swam away, he saw that it only stroked with one of its legs.

He must have broken the other in his tight grip. This gave him the pang that such a thing can give a boy who already has shot at least a dozen sparrows with his bb gun and can remember the light fading from the eye of one he held in his hand, demonstrating for him the art of dying.

He walked on, that day, looking at the ground, perhaps suspecting that such a time might stick with him. To walk from his house across a quarter mile of fields to the highway, and then down the long hill to the bridge over Town Creek, and then up the short hill to the bank and the one short block of stores would take him nearly an hour – it was not something he had done many times. That block of stores was called Court Street. Just past it was the movie theater, and on Saturday afternoons, beginning this season, James was allowed to make such a pilgrimage as this, looking down. Looking down at the rocks and cans and wobbling small appliances that sometimes studded the bed of Town Creek. Looking up at the fan belt display in the window of the auto parts store. Looking down at the cobble bricks that made up Fifth Street. Looking up Court Street at noon on Saturday, too early for the movie, another Western in which the bad guys seemed already to be played by the same actors (but wasn't that what gave so much satisfaction), looking sideways at the farmers' parked pickup trucks, the strolling families. But that would be later. Now the street was empty. After the movie let out, around four in the afternoon, the street would be crowded. James had time, at least an hour, to spend in Baker Brothers' Hardware Store. It was about halfway up the block, across from the Woolworth Five and Dime – the storefront was a little darker than its neighbors, a furniture store and one of the three town drugstores. There were pocketknives on display behind the dusty window, and lanterns.

There was an old dusty plaque or photograph with something about a Mosler Safe and Hiroshima. That was the atom bomb. All you had to do was get in a safe. But the storefront was not as dark as the inside. And then there were the two Baker brothers.

One was called Morris. James had heard his mother talking about him – that he was very old and sick and that his brother was older. But they were both always in the store. A short one (which James thought was Morris, but since they were both to be called Mr. Baker by a kid, it really didn't matter much), and a taller one. They both were old, indeed. Morris, if he was the short one, had some color left in his hair, but his skin was wrinkled and his eyes seemed to have the consistency of pudding. He might have smelled dusty, but the store itself would have covered that up.

Today it was the tall one who called him Jamie and asked after his mother who worked at the bank. Yes, Wallace, the tall one. Mr. Baker, too. My mother is fine James thought he said, sliding himself out from under the hand that lit in his hair like a bat, ready to crawl. The store was a place for looking: two aisles running toward the back. Above, the stamped tin ceiling was brown, a color that had once been another color and domed lights hung from it, only a few of which still lit. Perhaps there was a ladder tall enough somewhere James thought as he moved toward the fishing gear hung on the wall next to the drug store. Hooks and bobbers hung on the wall. Lead weights like bb's called split shot and then larger ones shaped like bells. Bobbers that were porcupine quills. Bobbers that were painted cork; then plastic, red and white, in sizes from sparrow's egg to baseball.

"Loose cattle?" Something from the voices near the front door causes him to pause.

"Just look at that. Jamie, come here." This is Wallace, who has only a dozen strands of hair lying across the top of his head. He thinks it's covered. James doesn't say this as he drags his feet. He was going to look at the flies. Tiny hooks and bristling fur. Black gnats and royal coachmen. He wants to buy the black gnat. There is nothing that flies or crawls around the ponds behind the clay mine that looks like the royal coachman. A coachman is a man in a costume who rides in a coach with horses. Or does he ride outside, watching the weeds wave by? James' father lets him ride on the fender of the car to open gates when they drive across pastures to fishing ponds. The weeds rake the sides of the car and the bottom of the car as it ploughs along the ruts. James opens the gates and closes them. Slipping loops of wire, sometimes untwisting them and twisting them back again. Like tying shoes.

"James, look out the door. Are you going to help or not?" It's Wallace holding the door open with a bat hand and Morris and that other bald man, the one that plays the organ at the Methodist Church, standing out on the walk. And there they go trotting by. Cows. Three of them. Little cows. What do you call them? Cattle. Steers. Calves. Loose cattle James thought meant something else. It means running loose. Bob, the man who plays the organ at the church, is telling Morris that the truck broke down and these calves escaped when they were supposed to go into another truck. Several men and boys are running up the street after them. Morris and Wallace and Bob are content to stand in front of the Baker Brother's Hardware Store.

"Where are they going?" James asks. Bob shakes his head. Even out here on the street, he smells like the Tap Room, the little stairway down into the basement of the Palace Hotel you pass on the way to the bakery. James starts to trot up Court Street. He sees a man holding on to the tail of one of the calves and the man begins shouting. Maybe it's the tails that are loose because the man falls down and the calf runs across the front lawn of the Baptist Church. James can hear Morris and Wallace and Bob behind him, their voices loud and excited. James turns around. He's never seen the Baker Brothers outside of their store together before. Morris has got his cane and he's moving along. Morris is loose.

James runs past the theater. He can't see the calves anymore. They were black and white like a snowy day with bright sun. This isn't a snowy day though. It's almost summer time. James thinks he hears voices from behind the Baptist Church so he runs down the side street and turns up an alley. He's never been here before. He slows down and he's breathing hard. Breathing goes faster but legs go slower James thinks with his hands on his knees. There are black cinders on the ground and a bottle cap for orange soda. There is also a nickel which is very hard to get out of the cinders but James manages after a while. Some of the cinders are sparkly. There is a sound that a calf makes, a cry, the kind they make when they want their mother. It's coming from way up Court Street. They can run too fast.

This is an alley with back yards and little sheds and woodpiles, firewood and brush. It's in the same block as the church but James has never been here before. It feels creepy. He trots back the way he came, the cross street with a big white house and a square stained glass window, and over to Court Street. Everybody must be chasing the cows. There isn't a soul in sight. And it's still way too early for the theater to open. James peers in the glass door of the theater. The red carpet is not all that clean. There are pieces of popcorn lying about, not whole pieces, but small white fragments. Mrs. Glenn must still be at home. Sometimes she is the only one in the theater on Saturday afternoons. She probably runs the projector, too.

Still nobody on the street. The door to Baker Brothers is standing open. James goes inside and closes the door. It has a string of bells which don't ring very loudly.

"Mr. Baker?" The place seems different. James' voice sounds like it belongs to somebody else. And there isn't any answer. Toward the back of the store there's a skylight and there is a patch of whitish light beneath it. It's not very bright because the skylight is small and it's dirty. James' mother has remarked upon the untidiness of the Baker Brothers' store, but what would a tidy hardware store look like? James is looking at the fishing lures. Hula poppers with long rubber skirts hanging around the deadly three-pronged hooks. Arbogast. James sounds out the word. Then there are torpedo-like brightly painted lures. Chuggers. Heddon. Another name to sound out. A picture of a jumping bass on the box. James has tried to draw this bass, starting with the open mouth. There are plastic lures with metal scoops fitted in the front. Jitterbug. This one floats and wobbles side to side, its spoon face fitted sideways. It makes a plopping sound that fish are supposed to like. Then, further toward the back of the store, something very large and bright green, six inches long, with three huge gangs of treble hooks. It looks like a fish with carefully painted scales and realistic eyes. It is magnificent. Musky Diver it says on the box. Muskellunge. James can't decide how to pronounce it. He reaches up to take it from the wall where it is fastened. Several other lures fall but the Musky Diver is stuck to something. James gives it a yank and a whole piece of the wall comes loose and tips toward him. The Musky Diver has come loose and James backs up, possibly a mistake, because there is nothing holding the tipping wall and it begins to fall, dropping bobbers and packages of hooks and sinkers. A whole display of metal spoons and spinners falls on a glass case and chimes musically. James has caught one of the hooks of the Musky Diver in his shirt and it has gone through to the barb. He can't get it out. It's a wonder he hasn't stuck the thing in his hand but now in his efforts to get it out of his shirt, he's got another one of the hooks snagged. The piece of wall was a board, like a blackboard with holes punched in it that was fastened there to display the fishing lures. Now it's caught on something, and most of the lures are still attached to it, and James realizes he is keeping it from falling the rest of the way. There is another board like this one and it has stringers, nets, and a whole display of dry flies, in an attached flat glass case. The piece of board that James is holding up with one hand while he struggles to unhook the Musky Diver with the other is still somehow connected to the other board on the wall and it seems to be pulling it away from the wall. There is a sound like someone unzipping a large zipper very slowly. It hasn't taken very long for all of this to happen, and even though there's no one yelling at him yet, James feels that hollow expectancy that comes before judgment. But now his heart is beginning to race as he realizes that he's got to make a decision about the piece of board he's holding on to.

Maybe he can push it back against the wall, but it's heavy and he still feels he'd better keep holding on to the Musky Diver to keep its sharp hooks out of his stomach. All three of the treble hooks are now securely biting into his shirt. He pushes with his shoulder against the board and it tips back toward the wall. There are still funny noises coming from the board with the glass fly case. Now he's got it upright. But the row of Hula Poppers was level with his shoulder and one of them is caught in his shirt sleeve.

"Great Scott, Jamie, what in the world have you got into?" James jumps and the Hula Popper hooked in his shirt comes off the wall. This is Bob, who might have removed his shoes the way he does when he plays the organ in the Methodist Church, to have sneaked up so silently. Bob has always seemed a serious man to James, but he's laughing now. His bow tie is moving up and down. James takes a step toward him and the zipping sound begins again from the board with the dry fly display case. It begins to tilt like a picture frame in an earthquake.

"Good heavens!" Bob lunges for the board and stops it from falling, pins it to the wall, and except for the tangle of metal fish stringers that have slid down his arms, nothing else is falling. James backs up until the board he was holding is leaning against Bob, and realizes that he is free.

"How did this happen? What were you doing?" Bob still has that grownup tone in his voice. He's going to know the reason why. Grownups always want to know the reason why.

"I wanted to see the Musky ..."

"What's happening?" It's Wallace, and his voice cracks when he's excited.

"Help me get this thing down off the wall or it's going to land on that glass case ...Wallace!"

Both Wallace and James are backing up. Wallace toward the front of the store, James toward the back. The display breaks loose and Bob jumps back at the same moment. The fish stringers are still tangled around Bob's arm and they pull the falling board away from the wall just far enough for it to fall, glass fly display against the standing glass case. There is a sickening crash, and the sound of breaking glass continues as objects keep falling into the standing case.

"I'm okay. I'm okay." Bob hops almost gracefully toward Wallace and the front of the store. James, still holding the Musky Diver away from his stomach, backs into the darkness beyond the skylight. The Hula Popper has fallen from his sleeve, but the Musky Diver has a death grip on the front of his shirt. He wonders about taking the shirt off. In the front of the store, Bob and Wallace are talking at the same time, like a radio that's not tuned in properly. Bob's looking to see if he has really cut himself, and Wallace's voice is cracking so much James can't understand what he's yelling. It's not easy to take off a shirt that's been gut-hooked by a six-inch fishing lure, James soon learns. He gives up and rolls the bottom of his shirt over the Musky Diver to provide a little camouflage. All this time he is backing away from the mid-store altercation, more and more deeply into the gloom. Maybe there's a back door. If this were the five and dime, this would be the place where the goldfish and the parakeets are. But it's not and it's really almost too dark to see. There's a desk and a chair. James is holding the lump in his shirt with one hand and reaching out with the other. And there's something white beyond the desk, a face. A dummy sitting in a chair. Bob and Wallace have gone out the front door into the light to check for splinters of glass, and this is a person, not a dummy, sitting back against the wall, eyes open.

"Mr. Baker?" It takes two tries for James to get his voice to work. This probably happens a lot to people when their hearts stop beating, James thinks.

Morris doesn't answer. It's not so dark now or else, somehow, it's getting easier to see. Morris is sitting with his hands clasped over a cane, looking over James' shoulder.

"Mr. Morris?" James would guess that Morris is taking a nap except for the way he is staring. He seems to be staring at the place where the musky Diver used to be displayed. He must be deep in thought. Or else ...

James extends his hand toward Morris Baker. Morris doesn't flinch. James' hand is shaking and it won't touch the hands holding the cane. It had been his plan, but his hand will have none of it. Morris might as well be behind a glass plate like the prairie dog display James saw once in a museum.

There is a back door, a loading dock, rickety stairs, an alley. In the bright sunlight, it's not all that difficult to disengage his shirt from three gangs of treble hooks. The shirt looks bad, but James has an established record of tearing his clothing climbing trees. It's like coming out of the movie theater. Here is a different world, light for dark. He doesn't hold a thing in his mind beside the bright hooked lure he holds in his hand. That frog in the mud visits him as a stray thought, but he blinks it away. He thinks of the way his Musky Diver will hook a pike. Shiny hooks grabbing the toothy lips, even the tongue and gills. That fish will be hooked for good, caught forever. Fish like to jump and spit the lure out, but not this one. James looks for a way to hide the thing – it's his now – a box from the trash bin, paper bag, something... . He's searching the ground. Bottlecaps, snail shells, nails. He'll find what he's looking for.

Now see him from above, the whole block of Court Street in the frame, not like a camera view, but like a drawing, everything a little out of true. There are men chasing calves along the frame. On the Court Street sidewalks, more people are walking now, not stick figures, either, and you can find the two in front of Baker Brother's hardware. One is holding his foot. It's done artfully. It's a picture that James himself will draw at school when he is supposed to be studying geography. It is geography, James thinks, and the man in front of the hardware store really looks like he's hopping.

When he finds this drawing again, James has gray hair. He's going through his mother's things. He looks at it, wondering. Neatly lettered below the hopping man are the words "Baker Brothers." There is an X over his own house on the map – it is certainly a map. He sees the carefully drawn calves running along Court Street. Now he has gone down to the basement of his mother's house, his father's house, where he has been sorting through the effects of their lives – and he finds it under the workbench, an old metal tackle box – when he opens that box, its hinges cry and complain a little. There are several tiers of trays that open outward. This was once an expensive purchase, but it proved to be too large to take on fishing trips. There – down in the bottom, tangled in a rusty stringer and a lump of half melted plastic worms – what he sees starts him remembering. As if a hand had reached down and grasped his whole body. Not unkindly but with too much strength.

Bad Starter

ometimes winning is the same as losing. James had quit his job in the orchestra and gone to Philadelphia where he found out what it was like to live in a place that rented for $30 a month and wasn't underpriced. After five years of interesting poverty, the opportunity to audition for the same orchestra arose. James took it, and he was offered his old job again. It was then that Anna told him she would not leave Philadelphia.

Anna gave him furniture and paintings. She was generous to a fault. And James found himself in that same small city in the South where he had started out eight years before. His friend Gerhard put him up for a week while he looked for a place to live. Eventually he found a small apartment in a larger house broken into three apartments. He had a view of a suburban street and of an ample, if weedy, yard where he would put in a vegetable garden under Gerhard's tutelage. The orchestra had fallen upon hard times and while the salary offered James a decent living, there was less work, fewer concerts. James was often at loose ends.

Gerhard was a French horn player and he lived in a large house with a woman named Doris. Doris was a good cook and Gerhard was an expansive Leo, always playing the generous host. James did not sicken and fail from eating his own cooking, but he was starved for company. Doris had lost custody of two children after a bitter divorce and congratulated James on the wisdom of not bringing children into his now failing marriage. (The phone calls to Anna were still frequent but there was less to talk about as it became clear Anna was not going to leave Philadelphia. Sometimes there was as much silence in a phone conversation as words.) There was little silence at Gerhard's house, however. There were always visitors and James became a regular dinner guest.

"I'm going to have to date," James said as he helped himself to mashed potatoes. Doris made them without peeling the potatoes and nobody but James ate more than one helping.

"Is there somebody you're interested in?" Doris asked.

"Nobody. I don't know where to start."

"How about your second flutist?" Gerhard frequently talked with his mouth full. "She'll probably consider it to be part of the job."

"Gerhard Hopkins," Doris said, "that woman is positively bony. You can see that James doesn't like her."

"I don't even like her playing," James said. "And even more to the point. She doesn't like me – 'the smell of beer on a man's breath is sexy,' she says, 'but not coming out of the end of a flute.'"

"Forget the bitch then. Just be sure to come to the park Saturday. We're going to fly kites. And there may be ladies present." Gerhard did his Groucho eyebrow exercise.

"Should I bring a kite?"

"Would you like to take those mashed potatoes with you? Nobody's going to eat them here."

* * *

James did bring a kite to the park, and before losing it in a tree he didn't notice was covered in poison ivy, he met a girl named Elise. She was a session musician, she said. Session violinists made a lot more money than symphony musicians, but they had to play boring music. Elise had short brown hair, very short, and she had high cheekbones. She was very active and cheerful and laughed often at remarks James made. And she was not bony like Sally the second flutist. James liked Elise.

Elise agreed to meet James at a little pub that evening. She gave him directions.

"That looks like poison ivy you're scratching," Elise said. "There's plenty of it on the tree – but thanks for trying to get my kite for me."

Why is it everyone knows how to identify poison ivy but me, James wondered, scratching some more. Elise hadn't seemed very sympathetic. She might have pointed it out before he climbed. It certainly was a healthy looking plant. Not a whit of bug damage.

Later, when James set out to go to Newton's Pub, his car wouldn't start. The starter was probably bad – he had just bought a new battery. Elise hadn't given him her phone number, and the conditions of their getting together were casual – he could stop by if he liked – she would probably be there. It wasn't really a date date.

Newton's was about a mile from James' apartment. He could walk. He looked over his garden as he set out. He had put in lettuce and radishes. The lettuce was coming up. It was already clear James was going to have more lettuce than he wanted. As he walked through his neighborhood, a dog in a parked car barked at him and startled him. It had waited until he had passed by and then launched a fusillade of furious barking and growling. James spun around and saw an animal much smaller than the sound of its barking suggested. Grateful he hadn't wet himself, James continued his walk, musing on the themes of portent and futility.

Newton's was farther than he had guessed. And there was something about walking that was more tiring than running. Maybe it was the tree climbing. Every intersection had lost pet posters attached to the telephone poles: lost wiener dogs, lost hairless cats, lost beagles. James stopped to read them all, resting from his journey. The posters all looked old – perhaps these pets had been found. Or maybe they had been abandoned in cars parked on the roadside where they terrorized passersby until they expired from starvation.

Inside Newton's, a little band was playing Irish music: a fiddle and a whistle player and two guitarists. James looked around for Elise but couldn't find her. When he was satisfied that she wasn't there, he sat down at the bar and ordered a Guinness. Just when he was ready to listen and enjoy the music, the musicians took a break. Then he saw Elise coming in the door of the pub – she walked by him on her way to the back, and she was with another person, holding hands with that person, in fact. And the person was a female person – a bony female person with dark short-cropped hair and a skull tattoo on her shoulder. James watched them pass by, apparently not noticing him. Had that really been Elise? Suddenly he couldn't remember what she looked like: Brown hair, high cheekbones – what color had her eyes been? Were they gray? Not blue – some lighter shade. Had this been a little joke? She was fading away. The little band began to play again, but the whistle was out of tune. Irish music all sounds the same, James decided as he trudged home.

In the next block James noticed a hand-painted sign in the window of a filling station that said *Honda Repair, Cal's Service*. It wasn't really a filling station anymore – the pumps had been ripped out and stacked against the side of the building, and there were about a dozen cars parked in close quarters – some, no, most of them were wrecked. The sign had a phone number. Maybe Cal could fix a starter. James tore a handbill about a lost cat off a telephone pole and wrote down the number. When he turned to walk the rest of the way home, he tripped on a thrust-up slab of sidewalk and nearly fell. It was an old handbill, James thought, years old, not really pet karma – nobody ever takes down handbills for lost cats.

The next morning James tried calling Cal's Service but there was no answer – he managed to get his Honda station wagon started, but the starter made some terrible noises before turning over. He decided to drive to Cal's Service. There was only one spot for him to park in – the place looked even less promising in the light of day. There was plywood in place of the front window, and the island where the gas pumps once stood looked positively dangerous, but the garage door was open and a single light burned toward the back. James stopped just inside the door.

"Hello."

The sound of a dropping wrench. A man, quite lame, emerged from the shadows, a short man, wiping his hands on a rag which was the same color as his coveralls, the color of oil, grease, barbeque sauce, blood – a man who had been dragged by life with one foot caught in the stirrup. He stood with his hip cocked, squinting at James, and saying nothing.

"I think I've got a bad starter. I wonder if you could look at it." James pointed toward his station wagon which was completely hidden by the junked armada.

Cal, if it was he, looked at James a moment longer, the rag forgotten in his hand. A muffled bark came from inside the station and James could hear a scrabbling sound coming from the door. Cal glanced at the door, then back at James.

"I thought you were somebody else," he said.

James couldn't think of a conventional response so he walked back through the maze toward his car. Limping profoundly, Cal followed him. When they got to James' car, Cal got in, turned off the ignition and then back on. Nothing happened.

"Bad starter," Cal said. "Cost you maybe $200."

"I haven't got that much," James said, aware that he no longer had a usable car. Cal looked at James with more interest. He had lank greasy hair, a great deal of it, and it, like the rest of him, was rumpled.

"Viet Nam." Cal said.

After another lengthy pause James realized it was a question. "No. Marine Band."

Cal's eyes brightened like a parrot and he rediscovered the rag he had been carrying. "Semper Fi," he said. "I can get you one off that Civic over there. A hundred bucks – professional courtesy."

"Well, when do you think you could get to it?"

"You got cash?"

"No, I'll have to write a check."

"Make it out to cash then. I've got a little issue." There was an outburst of barking from the station.

"Shut up, Mildred!" Cal spun around and started toward the garage, stopped suddenly, and without turning spoke again. "Come back in an hour and a half." And he limped away.

Enough time to walk home, turn around and walk back. James decided to wander around the neighborhood. A block away, Newton's Pub, the scene of his unsuccessful date with Elise, was not open. In fact, most of the storefronts were boarded up. There was a convenience store a block farther on and a working gas station. James bought a Coke. The next block contained a small park with a low stone wall bordering the sidewalk. James sat on the wall and finished his soft drink. At the end of the block James found a trashcan and noticed the corner house across the street which was the beginning of a more residential-looking area. *Madame Blavatasky, Fortunes Told, Notary Public.* Blavatsky? At least the sign was more professional than Cal's.

"Hello."

James started. The voice came from a girl of about nine, dressed incongruously in a dirty white party dress which featured lace and flounces. Likely it had its origin in a thrift store before it had apparently been worn to slide into home base in a softball game.

"Hello, yourself." James said.

"My name is Florence. What's yours?" The child was simple-minded, James decided.

"My name is James, but my friends call me Jimmy," James said.

"Oh." Florence had apparently exhausted the possibilities

of the conversation she had instigated. Perhaps, she, like Cal, had taken James for someone else.

"Do you live around here?" James asked.

"I live across the street." Florence pointed toward the Blavatsky sign house. Her voice seemed not to have inflection. James wasn't accustomed to talking to children, but he was almost certain that Florence shouldn't be alone in the park striking up conversations with loitering strangers.

"Shouldn't you be at home, then?"

"I'm afraid to cross the street."

"Well, then, let me help you." James did not take Florence by the hand, but he walked to the street corner, and she followed. "There aren't any cars coming now. Let's cross now," James said. This time a warm, sticky hand took his.

Florence did not relinquish James' hand as he walked up the steps to the front door. There, another sign hung which said *Open, Walk In.* James continued, Florence positively hanging on. A string of elephant bells jangled, and while James might have expected incense, he was greeted with a heavy smell of cooking, cabbage or Brussels sprouts. The sticky hand let go. And there was music in this rather ordinary sitting room, Patsy Kline singing a song James simply couldn't stand, "Crazy" – someone had made a string arrangement of it for the orchestra and, as a consequence, he had been its captive audience on dozens of occasions.

"Flo, why you are so late?" From the next room. What kind of accent was that? Eastern European? Russian? Fake? There was no crystal ball, no beaded curtains. Patsy Kline abruptly ceased with the distinctive signature of a needle slipping on vinyl. "Oh, I beg your pardon. I didn't realize I have customer." The voice belonged to a woman who might have been Flo's grandmother. She had a heavy face and her hair was a brunette lump about the size of a sleeping cat. A red housedress and red bunny slippers completed her ensemble. Maybe the cat-sized hair was a wig, James thought.

"Florence came up to me in the park – she said she was afraid to cross the street." There was a small walnut table in the center of the room and two chairs opposite each other. This must be the playing field. On the walls, some photographs. Family groupings, studio posed. No gurus with flowing beards. No crystal ball.

"Florence, thank you to the gentleman," the woman said, lowering herself into one of the chairs. She was no more overweight than the average grandmother, James thought – but her skin was puffy and her eyes deep-set. She grunted and the chair squeaked in commensurate complaint.

"Thank you, Jimmy," Florence said and stood expectantly.

"Florence, you may be excused," the woman said. Then to James: "Did you come for the fortune?"

"Actually, I'm waiting for my car to be repaired down the block – and when Florence asked me to help her cross the street…"

"Your aura is damaged. You do need to see the fortune."

"My aura?"

"A leaking boat will sink –"

"My aura is leaking?"

The woman said nothing, giving James a sad smile.

"Listen, I have a bad starter, and it's going to cost $100. No. There's a guy over there in the next block whose name is Cal and he's giving me a professional discount because I was in the Marine Corps. But right now he can't find the tool to get the starter off an old Civic. No, there's going to be a bolt that's seized, and he won't have it ready. I'll have to walk home. How's that for my fortune?"

"My name is Madame Blavatsky," the woman said with great dignity, laying her hands, palms downward on the little walnut table. "Sit down for the fortune. It is what you say. Your car will not be ready. And tomorrow he will charge you $150."

"There was a Madame Blavatsky, a historical figure…" James began.

"Yes, I have chosen my name. Let me see the hands. Sit down." James relented. "Is Florence…"

"Florence brings in my customers. Florence is my familiar." James withdrew his hands from her grasp.

"Good heavens. You have no…" She closed her eyes in concentration. "…no place to take the joke." She gave James a big smile and he could see her teeth were very even and an unnatural shade of white. "Now we can see the problems. Give me those hands. Flo is a grandchild – a neighbor child – I have a border who lives…" She gestured toward the ceiling. "…up the stairs. Which do you like best?"

James submitted to having his hands turned palms up and palms down repeatedly, impatiently.

"You are musician. You have lost a wiener dog. No. Dogs bark at you. Many dogs." She shook her head in annoyance. "There is a woman. Now this is difficult. A tattoo? No. Some kind of mark. A scar – a birthmark, perhaps. On her neck." She shrugged.

"A violinist or a violist," James said, "would have a mark on her neck. It comes from the instrument. But I don't know anybody. I've only been in town a month."

"Yes, you know anybody. And you take the joke. There on your arm. That is poison ivy. I see a kite."

James looked at her in surprise.

"Yes, see, shape of a kite." She pointed again to the red patch on James' arm – it was indeed kite-shaped.

"I climbed a tree," James said. "To get a kite. And there was somebody – I guess there was a joke – but how did you peg me as a musician?"

"Most of my customers are musicians. Why shouldn't you? And you're not from here. You don't talk like here."

She laughed at James' quizzical expression. "I, too, am not from here."

James began to push his chair back.

"No, no. Now the tarot cards. Stay." This last command might have caused a whole kennel of disobedient dogs to hold their ground.

Madame Blavatsky rushed out of the room muttering in a language James did not recognize. There had been a sound, a disturbance. Florence reaching for cookies, James thought. The old lady had put him in a seeing mode. Cal working a wrench and skinning his knuckles. Gerhard and Doris, over coffee, saying his name, speaking of Anna. The word "foolish." Fortune telling was rife in this room. The Sears family photos had auras: pink and red. In the corner, a rocking chair with a carved back seemed to move, but when James focused his stare, recanted. Just furniture, the room insisted. On the mantel, a few painted plates held up by little metal stands languished. Behind the door from which had issued the commotion, silence.

James got up and brushed imaginary dust from his pants legs. He could tell the door was going to open. A procession: Florence in a clean white frock carrying something apparently heavy and rectangular, covered with white cloth, and following, Madame

Blavatsky. Florence carefully set the object down on the table and stepped back smiling.

"Not the tarot," said Madame B. "Please to sit."

James sat. No tarot, and not cookies, James thought. So much for prescience.

Madame B nodded to Florence and Florence lifted the cloth. Before James, a small terrarium, and in it, five, no, six mice. Brown and white and much agitated, crawling over one another. They were neither cute nor repulsive. They were mice.

"Eee eee," said Florence, and Madame B made a notation in a small notebook. She had a stubby pencil like the ones James remembered from miniature golf.

"Eee eee eee," said Florence. Another notation.

One of the mice seemed to have disengaged itself from the general melee and was sniffing the glass or the plastic in James' direction. Was it pressing its face against the glass?

Florence continued with her Morse code and Madame B her dictation.

James watched the mouse watching him, the old lady and the child with growing consternation. He had not smoked any dope this morning. He didn't think he had smoked the day before, but now he wasn't certain.

"No eee," said Florence.

"No eee?" said Madame Blavatsky.

"What in the world are you doing?" said James, pulling his chair away from the milling mice.

"Florence has good ear," said Madame B. "She can hear the mice talk."

"She can hear the mice," James heard himself repeat numbly.

"Very old way – the mice talk of the future – we call myomancy – now wait." The old woman went to a small bookcase James hadn't noticed before and brought forth a small book with cracked leather binding and began carefully leafing through it while making further notes with her baby pencil. Florence carefully covered the mice. The door to the kitchen (it was the kitchen) had been left open and James inhaled a nauseating wave of boiling cabbage.

"Good smell, no," said the old lady, looking up from her calculations.

"We don't cook the mice," Florence said. This was intended to be helpful, James decided.

"Why so white the face? Afraid of mice?" Madame B chuckled for a moment – then returned to her calculations.

"Not good." She said.

"What's not good?"

"The woman. The mice say not good. You stay away the woman with the tattoo."

"That won't be difficult," James said. "But I've got to ask you – you, Florence. What is 'no eee'?"

Florence shrugged.

James looked at the woman with the red bunny slippers.

"She never say before 'no eee.'"

"I think they were holding their breath," Florence said. "I can hold my breath for a long time. Want to see?"

James could see the cabbage boiling and seething. He could taste sulfur.

"I've got to go. Thank you for the fortune, Madame Blavatsky. But I don't feel well – I've got to get some air."

He took out his wallet: all he had was a five and two ones. He laid the two ones on the table. Then picked them up and replaced them with the five. Then added the two ones. Madame B and Florence stood in silent tableau. Careful of the elephant bells, he opened the front door and let himself out. The door opened behind him. Florence overtook him.

"She says to bring a twenty next time," Florence said.

The day was getting hot. The park was deserted – no more miniature Emily Dickinsons. At Cal's Service, James' presence in the garage door set off a fusillade of barking from the station and brought Cal soon after, slouching and tacking.

"All done, and I can charge you $90," Call said, or seemed to say, because the barking persisted.

"Only $90?" James regretted his lapse immediately, because Mildred had ceased her racket. Had they been in a crowded restaurant rather than a dark garage, heads would have turned. Cal looked pained. He turned and went to the station door.

"Come on and I'll write you up. Don't come close to the desk and Mildred will leave you be." Inside the station there was more light. A double row of fan belts hung along the back wall, carefully arranged from small to large, so the effect was of a fan belt crescendo. Every surface was covered with grease or with grease covered with dust and sitting in a chair behind the desk, almost hidden in a pile of coveralls and other clothing, was a medium-sized snarling dog. A brown dog, a ragged, tattered, autumnal dog. Mildred's snarl was sustained *sotto voce*, suggesting a patient animosity, one which might be satisfied only when James turned to leave. He resolved never to turn his back on the likes of Mildred.

"Ninety dollars made out to cash," Cal reminded James, as he rummaged through miscellaneous items on the desk top, the most incongruous of which was a framed photo of a younger Cal and a child, bookended by two oil cans.

James wrote out the check and Cal handed him a smudged illegible bill, accidently knocking over the photo and then carefully, fastidiously righting it.

"Ever have a runaway?" he asked, now holding back Mildred who seemed to sense James' resolve not to undertake a blind retreat. "Just last week. I heard the dog and took off after him. He took maybe $300 – a lot of money. 1:30 at night, I spotted him off the freeway, just short of the Nations, you know, the projects. I spun out, left my door open, chased him three blocks. Key in my hand, I'm no fool. Damn kid got away. Fifteen years old and five inches taller than his dad."

"I don't have any kids," James said, beginning to back away.

"Sorry about the dog. She's just old and mean. Keeps me safe, not that there's anything anybody..." He broke off and gave the dog a little shake which caused her to pause and wheeze for breath.

"Thanks, then," James said.

His starter, his new starter, sounded odd, like a cat with a furball, but the car started.

"Hey James." A voice James has heard before. "Want to go kite flying?" This is Elise. She seems cheerful enough, walking from the direction of the park. "What happened last night? You never showed up."

James is sitting in his Honda with the motor running on the outside edge of Cal's used car lot / cemetery. He rolls the window down the rest of the way. "I thought – I guess I – well, it's a long story. Do you live around here?"

"No. I come down here once in a while to get my fortune

told. Back there – corner house. There's this really strange old lady, but she's good. She told me where my ring was when I lost it. And she's got this little kid who's even weirder than she is."

Elise has a grip on the bottom of the window. She is either very relaxed or getting ready to write James a ticket. He wants to get out of the car but can't figure out a way. He can see the violin mark on her neck.

"That's the thing," she says. "She told me you were heading over this way to this – she gestured vaguely, distastefully – this place. She said I should tell you something. That it wasn't me you saw. Who did you see?"

James shakes his head slowly.

"No, that's not all," Elise says. "There was something about a tattoo. Darn. Now I can't remember. Sometimes she gets excited and she's hard to understand. It was like 'don't do the tattoo' or 'do the tattoo.'"

The Honda has been idling. James turns the ignition off.

"I don't really want to fly kites," Elise says. "Do you want to come over to my place and hang out? Yeah?" James wonders if he has given up some secret through his body language. He's given it up, but he doesn't know what it is.

I'm in a red Morris Minor parked two blocks up, across from Madame Blavatsky. You can follow me. We'll have fun." Elise smiles, lewdly, James thinks, and then she turns and jogs, practically dashes back down the street. James watches her very attractive rear end as she moves away. She has a very athletic gait, very upright and graceful.

Time's wasting. James turns the key in his ignition. Nothing happens. He sighs, leans back in his seat. The time not yet wasted slows down. He can see down the block – past a telephone pole with at least three lost pet signs on it – a small red car pulling into the street, hesitating – then driving away.

Basswood Bend

Early spring. Only a few kinds of trees in blossom. Pear. The ones that always split in a high wind, and maybe cherry, James couldn't be sure. The trees were completely bare around Basswood Bend where he was moving his things into the Basswood Apartments. His landlady had been true to her word. She gave him a chance to buy the little house on Ashland Circle. But he had no money saved and the Symphony tended to go on strike or be locked out it seemed every other year. And the thick chocolate wall to wall carpet in the new apartment would be a lot safer for little Andrew, the two-year old he co-parented. Gwen had moved out less than a year after Andrew was born. It had been a harrowing home birth, but that was Gwen's style. This was her week with the child, so he had time to unpack and get settled.

This was the last load, boxes of music. They were more work than the over-sized filing cabinet that contained them – that slid on the thick carpet like a sled in Chekov. Even up the stairs. James had managed it by himself.

Now he looked across the parking lot toward a dumpster, a row of bare trees about as tall as he was, and one solitary daffodil. A scout, perhaps. Maybe this place wouldn't be this ugly in a few more weeks. James could smell the river – it was on three sides of the apartment complex, no more than a few blocks away. It wasn't an entirely pleasant smell. James hefted a boxload of over-sized Anderson etudes and narrowly avoided stepping on a dead mole as he rounded the corner to the walkway that led to his apartment.

"Sorry about that." A voice startled him. "I poison them and the cats drag them around." A large man in shorts and tee shirt, a rag tied around his head, rough looking. James thought of the convict in *Great Expectations*. But this character was standing in the doorway of his apartment. Barefoot. At least, no leg irons.

T. R. McDermott," he announced. "You can call me Junior. All the ladies call me Junior. Welcome to Basswood Bend, named for the trees they cut down to build this apartment complex." And he held out his hand, oblivious to the fact James was hanging on to a large box of music.

James set the box down on the sidewalk, next to the dead mole.

"I'm James," he said, straightening up. Maybe this guy worked at the prison. He had something that could have been a knife scar across his forehead.

"James Baxter." James survived the handshake. He had expected to be crushed.

"Well, you got to move in. I seen you and your buddies carrying in your stuff. You don't have much stuff."

James thought about that – he had a Navy surplus writing desk and a round maple table, a few chairs for it, a TV and baby toys – maybe Andy had more stuff than he did.

"We'll get to know each other I expect. Here you go." And Junior picked up the box with little effort and handed it to James.

"So you're some kind of musician?"

"I play in the orchestra, the Symphony."

"The Sympathy? Damn, I can't say that."

"You play a violin?" He said the word slowly and carefully.

"Flute," James said.

"Flute," Junior said thoughtfully. Then again, "Flute."

James shifted the box of music to get a better grip, and when he looked up Junior had stepped back into his apartment and shut the door, like a cuckoo retreating into its clock.

James spent the rest of the day restoring the music to the big cabinet. There were four big sliding shelves that could be pulled out: methods and etudes on the top. He wondered if he could get any private students to come this far out of the city. The rent wasn't bad but there was only one road. The only way in if you don't count the ferry. And the nearest attraction was a prison – better to worry about teaching later. Orchestral excerpts on the bottom shelf. Look at this: Wagner operas. He had bought that book before he knew how to pronounce Wagner. Pretty much a waste. But the flute part in the Siegfrid Idyll is nice. For James, looking through music was like throwing away newspapers. You can't help stopping to read. And when he was done there was a litter of yellowed corners broken from the pages. Some of the French music was already old when he bought it. Vintage fantasies and variations on opera themes. Verdi's *Macbeth*. An assortment of Carnivals of Venice. Did he know the flute was all bubbles and feathers when he picked it out?

James decided to play some of the old pieces after he had finished stocking the music cabinet. The carpet soaked up sound and muffled the flute tone. But after a while he had adjusted, blowing harder, breathing faster. Variations on breathing. That's why angels play harps. They can't breathe. But no, they play trumpets and post horns. You don't say Gabriel blow your flute.

Somebody was at the door, banging away at the knocker. It sounded determined rather than angry, James thought. Probably he hadn't heard it at first. He was sorry to put the flute down. He had been sounding pretty good. Nobody knows what it feels like except, well, every other flute player in the world. But not some of his students.

At the door then. Magwitch. Who else?

"Sorry to bother you at your playing."

Junior had added flip-flops to his attire. And he was carrying a box with a keyhole and a key sticking out of it. It had once been covered with leather, but precious little of that remained. It was old, maybe an old instrument case. James took all this in while Junior stood there staring at the box he was now holding with both hands. It seemed to have completely distracted him from his mission.

"Come in," James said, beginning to feel annoyed. Junior smelled like stale cigarette smoke and something else, something in the feet family. James backed up to give him room to enter, and to get away from the smell.

"My old dad gave me this, " Junior said. "I had a hell of a time finding it. I haven't kept my place as neat as this."

Junior walked over to James' best piece of furniture, the maple dining room table, and set the box on the table. Then he looked at James expectantly. He didn't seem as threatening as he had by the mole. But what did he want? Had he just delivered a pizza?

"It's an old flute," Junior said. "My dad used to play it before he lost his teeth. I just wondered if it still works. I was thinking I'd take it up."

Astonishing. "Well, let's have a look," James said. He worked the key back and forth until, eventually, the case lid released. Inside was an old style, six-keyed wood flute. It was not blackwood or ebony. The wood was a light brown – perhaps cocuswood or boxwood. The keys were much tarnished but appeared to be real silver. James took out the headjoint.

"Here's the problem," James said, feeling almost completely relieved now that he had a flute in his hands. "See the tuning barrel? It's got a metal lining. Over time the wood dries out and shrinks. The metal doesn't. So the wood cracks. This one is cracked all the way through."

"It's ruined then?" Junior's voice showed real disappointment.

"Maybe, maybe not. A real repairman might be able to fix it permanently. But I can try something I used to do with my wood flutes. I don't suppose you have any clear fingernail polish."

Junior gave him a look.

"Well, I've got some with my repair kit. It's not unpacked is the thing. If you leave the flute with me I'll try to fix the crack. Then we can see if it will work. But you can easily get a modern flute at a music store. You can even rent one for next to nothing."

"I want to play my dad's flute," Junior said. "He used to play old timey tunes. I think I can remember some of them. They wouldn't sound right unless they came out of this here flute."

"Why don't you leave it with me and I'll try to patch it up for you when I find the clear polish?"

"I'll get the polish." Junior took the headjoint from James, placed it gently in the box, closed the lid and turned the key. The key reminded James of a windup toy. "And I'll fix it, too." He sounded belligerent again.

Junior strode toward the front door, releasing a wave of cigarette and foot scent, pulled it open, paused, then turned around.

"Is it different to play than the kind you play?"

"The fingerings are different, but not too much. It's like a baroque flute,"

"Broke is right." Junior made a peculiar sound, a wheeze or cough – perhaps he was laughing.

"Tell you what. If you show me how to hold it and what the notes are, I'll give you a beer." Not waiting for an answer, he popped out the door and half-slammed it behind him.

"Well," James said, perhaps to the brown carpet.

* * *

The concert had been gratifying. Dvorak's 4th Symphony is full of tuneful flute solos and the orchestra's recent financial distress had a silver lining. Rehearsals and concerts were now in a smaller hall with much better acoustics. The "new" hall had been terrible, no better than the room with the brown shag carpet. James drove by Gwen's apartment to pick up Andrew. The sleeping child didn't wake while James carried him to his car and strapped him into his baby seat. Not wanting to hear any more music, James found a college basketball game on the radio and drove along almost deserted

Charlotte Avenue thinking about how baseball works on the radio and basketball doesn't. Baseball presents a situation. Basketball is like a flock of birds turning and twisting in the wind. Realizing he was speaking aloud, James turned off the radio.

"It's not that there's anything wrong with talking to yourself, Andy," he now addressed his sleeping child. "I know you do it all the time. It's a sign of an active mind, an active imagination." Andrew continued sleeping.

"Remember that skunk we saw last summer when I was carrying you to the car after a concert? You were sleeping then, too. I couldn't very well yell, 'Skunk, Skunk,' at the top of my lungs so you could wake up and see. Skunks don't like to be startled. So I stopped and waited for the skunk to go on and do its skunking somewhere else. Skunks skunk and Andy sleeps. And James drives home from concerts in the night. Maybe this is the best time. Some good work behind me, and all the street lights trying to get behind me, too. Did you ever notice that?"

The Basswood Bend complex was mostly dark. James had called the girl he had been seeing recently and invited her to come over after the concert. Her name was Jill and she was a dancer. He had left a message and she hadn't returned it. Not likely she would turn up. Jill was not a ballet dancer but a modern dancer. She had about the same build as a tennis player. Still, it would be exciting to make love to a dancer. James had seen her company perform. There was a lot of running around and sudden stopping. And the music was one guy who could play fiddle and guitars. He was actually more interesting than the dancers.

James and Jill were barely past the coffee together stage. Jill didn't seem very enthusiastic about the relationship, but she was good with Andy. She seemed to like Andy more than James, but maybe that's her way of showing affection – friendship – whatever. James pulled into a parking place as close to his apartment as he could. Somebody had parked an old white pickup directly in front. He hoisted the sleeping child so his chin rested shoulder high. Andy in one hand, flute bag in the other.

Then at the door he put the bag down and was trying to get his keys out of his pocket on the wrong side. Andy was getting big and you have to bend yourself awkwardly to keep him upright. James had never dropped him but came close once when he was a baby.

"James."

Of course he jumped and dropped the keys which were almost fitted in the lock.

"I'll take him." Jill had a breathy voice which James liked a lot. And he liked the way she smelled. She said once it was a man's cologne.

"I didn't think you'd come," James said after getting the lights on and taking still-sleeping Andy from Jill.

James put Andy down in his room upstairs. He left the night light on and the door cracked. When he went downstairs Jill was gone. Then there was a little tap at the door.

"I brought you a bottle of wine. I had to get it from the truck."

"That truck is yours? Do you do construction for your day job?" Jill didn't smile. But she looked good. Her hair was short but tousled in some kind of intentional way that looked really sexy. And she had the whitest smoothest skin which James hoped he might get to see more of later that night.

"We had a late rehearsal," she said, "and I figured your concert was going to be over soon – I didn't have to wait long. The truck's a longer story. I ran into an old friend recently. An old flame, I guess."

James sat down, suddenly tired. "An old flame."

"Sorry about the timing."

"And you're moving in with your old friend."

Jill took the bottle into James' kitchen and found a bottle opener in the silverware drawer.

"And you brought me a bottle of wine as a going away present."

"You're a smart guy. Here's to you. Actually, I'm moving away from the city, but not that far. And I'm not moving in with my old friend. But I might, eventually. I guess. This is his truck. Anyway, I don't think you want to talk about it. It's just not the right time for us. I thought it might be. You got any dope?"

James shook his head.

"Well, I do. Roll us a joint."

"I'm not sure I see the point."

"The point is a little wine, a little smoke, and your going away present."

"You're suggesting pointless, empty sex?" James asked as he took the pack of cigarette paper from his flute case he used to keep the pads dry.

"Well, think of it as friendly."

And it was friendly, but more than a little awkward. It takes time, James reflected, to get the angles right. At least the dope made it go slow. Then she dressed herself – such a sad thing, he thought, a woman putting on her clothes after making love. Suddenly he wanted to catch her up and undress her again – she probably would have tolerated it. But he didn't. He watched her practiced movements and thought about how she was strange only to him, not to herself. He felt something slipping away from him, her strangeness perhaps. An ache began. It's my heart, he thought. It's cracking.

"Good night, and thanks for the wine," James said. "Thanks for everything."

She kissed him.

"You always had good manners."

After Jill left, James went into Andy's room and straightened the blanket around him. He would be awake early.

* * *

Andy liked to empty his Lego blocks out of their container and then put them back in, one after another. He sang to himself as he dropped the little plastic pieces, then he dumped them out again. Gwen was sure he was not developing properly. The pediatrician was comforting, but Gwen would not have any of it. James watched him playing with the blocks. He could feel the crack widening and closing as he breathed. Something was leaking out of him. "It's just hope," he said aloud. Andy stopped singing and looked at him, smiled, and went back to sorting.

* * *

After the rehearsal, James picked up Andy from Mrs. Joyce. Mrs. Joyce lived across the street from the house James had rented. Before he took over the lease it had been his old girlfriend Sharon's house. And she had left him for an old lover. James thought about this while Mrs. Joyce prattled on about Andy's adventures. The same story, he thought, but more dramatic. He had not cracked then. He split down the middle. A pattern? Of course there was a pattern. Theme and variations.

At home he found a note taped to his door. It was completely illegible but the signature might be Junior. He had to get Andy ready for Gwen to pick him up. Junior could wait.

Andy was usually pretty good about the changing of the guard, but this time he cried and clung. Gwen accused James of giving him candy. Probably Mrs. Joyce had fed him something she shouldn't. Finally the whole circus was out the front door and the red Celica drove away. James noticed she had a dangerously low tire and tried to flag her down, but she either didn't see him or purposely ignored him.

Giving Andy over to Gwen was stressful on a good day. James got a beer out of the refrigerator, turned on the news and eased himself into the butterfly chair.

Loud knocking at the door. What had he forgotten to pack in the baby bag? But this was Junior, the convict from the marshes. He had used his bandana to tie around his flute case, a sign of some arcane progress, perhaps.

"James, did you get my note?" Junior brushed past him and took his flute case to the maple table.

"There was a note on my door, but I couldn't read it."

"That's what happens when you're left handed and they make you learn to write with your right hand," Junior said, untying the bandanna. "Here it is. Does it work?"

James took the flute out of the box and assembled it. The crack in the tuning barrel had been filled with nail polish. It wasn't completely dry and it smelled strongly.

"The joints have got string wrapped around them," Junior said. "I asked at the music store and they gave me a little tin of cork grease. No bigger than a quarter. So you should be able to put it together."

James carefully assembled the body parts of the flute.

"Well, let's see if I can get a sound out of it." James picked it up and blew what should have been a G. Nothing came out. Not a weak or deformed sound. Nothing at all.

"Oh shit," opined Junior.

James, puzzled, removed the headjoint and peered through the body of the flute. It was a perfect spyglass. James blew on the headjoint. Nothing.

"There's something stuck inside the headjoint," James said, working his finger into the tube. "I think I can just reach it." It was a plastic sandwich bag containing a small amount of something that looked a great deal like..."

"My dope!" Junior exclaimed. "I got messed up and hid it. I guess I forgot where."

James gave him the baggy and reassembled the flute.

This time he blew and the flute sounded – it didn't sound bad. He played down the scale to the lowest note, D. It sounded strong.

"You did it, Junior," James handed him the flute. "It works."

"Only thing is I can't play it."

"Did you ever blow over the top of a soda bottle and get a hooty noise?"

Junior nodded.

"Take the headjoint off the flute and look at yourself in that mirror on the door. This is where the flute goes on your lip. Now blow. No. Hold the sides of your lips together. Think sardonic smile. If that doesn't work, think cat's asshole."

Junior wheezed. That was it, then, his way of laughing.

Then tried again. Finally. A sound.

"That's all there is to it. It will be more difficult when you put the whole flute together. See where your fingers go? You can actually play this kind of flute left handed but then you wouldn't be able to use the keys. First get the left hand notes. Think of it as the top hand. You can get a tin whistle at the music store. It will have the same fingerings. Work out tunes on the whistle, then try them on the flute."

Junior forgot he had promised James a beer. He was so delighted with his flute he went directly home. James noticed he had forgotten the baggy of marijuana.

"To the teacher go the spoils," James said, and he rolled himself a fat number, put on Glen Gould's Goldberg Variations and smoked the whole thing. There were about three fingers of Jill's wine left. He drank a toast to her.

Feathers

ommy is sitting in his once comfortable desk chair. He is thinking about the wisteria that isn't blooming on either side of his front porch. The dog has broken into a fine flop behind him. They (the man and the dog) are at the balance point of a day that began full of rain and has now dried out. There are buds and tiny leaves on the crepe myrtles, the vitex, and the redbud. In his back yard, both Japanese maples have begun making their small elaborate leaves. Tommy is a fiction writer and he's making a living teaching others. He's mostly working at staying in his once-comfortable chair, trying to get words on a page. Tommy's wife Elsa is a teacher. She teaches in a community college and teaches all the humanities courses. Tommy can't call it a good job. It comes with a decent salary, but it's more the calling of a saint.

Tommy has a few students who might be thrilled to touch his robe and he wouldn't mind having a beer with a few others of them but they all live on the west coast or Paris or Switzerland or Uzbekistan.

Elsa comes home from teaching.

"There's a burglar in the kitchen," Tommy says to the dog who dutifully hops down from the pillowed antique campaign frame she was sleeping on. In the kitchen Elsa is unpacking the containers that organized her elaborate lunch.

"June and Gene tonight," Tommy says.

"Shit."

"I believe you've nailed the subtext," Tommy says. "We can take a big bottle or two of wine. I can still drive with one eye closed."

"Does he still smoke cigars?"

"I forgot about that. I said we'd come at six –June is cooking. I remember she's a pretty good cook."

"Probably vegan."

"I checked his directions. There's a Wendy's and a Burger King on the way."

Tommy notices he is alone in the kitchen with the dog. Elsa has gone into the bedroom, perhaps to change. The dog is looking up at Tommy intently, chewing on a mouthful of kibble. It is her habit. A piece drops to the floor. Tommy retrieves it and replaces it in the dog food dish.

*   *   *

"There it is. Ranch. Just like the other."

"Don't park in the driveway. Somebody might park us in."

"Right, better to get tanked up and fall in the ditch." Tommy and Elsa have actually fallen in a ditch, but neither of them can remember the actual fall.

"What is that?" Elsa says.

"It's a concrete goose, just like Gertie." Tommy and Elsa stare at a hand-painted cast-concrete porch ornament which is wearing a nice spring outfit with an Easter basket and a straw hat. It has blue eyes, a yellow beak, and even carefully painted eyelashes.

"Let's get out..."

"Hey, maestro. Long time no see." Gene has not so much burst out of a cloud of cigar smoke as he has dragged it along with him like a wall cloud hiding a tornado.

The wall cloud dissipated. Gene used to smoke Cuban cigars. He had once persuaded Tommy to try one. But then, isn't a cigar almost always just a cigar? Inside, June seemed a tad more matronly, but time had treated her more kindly than Gene. He was a wreck.

"You're looking good, June," Tommy said. "Like your Facebook photos – book jacket portraits every one."

"Gin," Gene said.

Tommy looked around. June and Elsa had gone into the kitchen. "Gin?"

The empty room offered no answer, but a large bird perched on the mantel emitted a rather unpleasant croaking sound. Tommy had not noticed it before it called attention to itself. It was quite black and had an unruly bunch of feathers at its throat.

The following is difficult to reproduce in the form of words written on paper. Gene said, "We're drinking gin," and Tommy said, "Is that a raven?" Simple declarative sentences but spoken at exactly the same time.

The raven took the occasion to ruffle its feathers and then to appear both relaxed and alert.

"Here, Thomas," said June, who had reentered the room and extended to him a tall glass of something clear and cold. "To old times."

Tommy glanced at Elsa, who was holding a similar glass in both hands and sipping from it the way a toddler might enjoy a glass of milk. She looked at him with an intimate, yet unforgiving expression. It might well have to do with that expression, *old times*.

"We'll be having ribs, but it would be nice to sit down and catch up," June said. Perhaps she said it sweetly.

"I was wondering," Tommy said, after settling himself in an unfortunately low riding easy chair, "about that turkey on the mantel. Is it wild or domestic?"

"His name is Henry," Gene said, sighting along his cigar at the impressive bird. "He is my familiar."

Henry, apparently knowing his name, did a little bird move in which feathers made him seem momentarily larger.

"I raised him from a chick," Gene said.

"Did he come rapping at your chamber door?" asked Tommy.

"Hey you guys, he's a pet," said June. "When April died, we thought at first we'd get another dog, but there's this place online. I wanted an owl, a barn owl, but you had to wait. Henry was ready to go. He doesn't fly and he doesn't talk. At least, not yet. And if you don't get too close to him, he doesn't bite. Cheers, Henry."

June toasted the creature, and so, too, did the company of friends, to a man, grateful to have something to do.

Gene paced into the kitchen and returned with a bottle of

gin which he splashed in glasses held out to him in much the same spirit as the previous toast.

"The world will need its poets," he said. "To us."

Tommy had managed to prize himself out of his low chair without spilling his gin – perhaps it had been gin and tonic originally. He felt light headed.

"Why Henry?" Elsa shot him a vicious look which he ignored. "Why not Mr. Bones?"

"Henry was my brother's name." Gene poured the rest of the gin into his own glass.

"That's a long sad story," said June. "Let's make plates and take them out into the backyard. It's warm enough – we can watch the fireflies and there's a wood thrush you can hear sometimes – I've never seen it. Reclusive character."

"So many birds..." Tommy began but Elsa caught him with a sharp elbow.

Finding himself alone with Henry, Tommy tried again: "I'd have thought a hermit thrush. But I'm no birder."

Henry croaked a little *sotto voce* croak and Tommy moved a little closer to the mantel. "Say again?"

Something odd was going on with Henry's pupils.

"Among twenty snowy mountains," Tommy began, "the only moving thing was the eye..."

Henry did not move all that quickly. And Elsa had already entered the room, sensing mischief. Tommy felt the kind of pain that causes men to speak in tongues, and perhaps he did.

"Why did you do that?" asked Elsa through clinched teeth as she wrapped Tommy's hand with the gauze June had produced, almost immediately.

"See how freely I'm bleeding," Tommy said. "No danger of infection."

"My brother died when the tractor fell on him," Gene offered, conversationally. "He tried to climb a hillside. We didn't find him until after dark. There were thousands of fireflies."

A bloody raven bite will often put a seal on an evening's activities but the gin had awakened appetites.

June carried a plate to the backyard picnic table for Tommy, and Gene remained subdued. He had even misplaced his cigar.

"Tommy, you're getting barbecue sauce all over yourself ," Elsa complained, not setting a better example.

A wood thrush called from the distance.

"There. That's it," said June. " Isn't it lovely?

Everybody listened because no one else had heard the thrush. Tommy stopped chewing. It was getting dark. The wood thrush was apparently a watched pot.

"Well, he's done singing," said June.

Everyone sat a while longer, contemplating the bird's silence. Sometimes, in the suburbs, a dog will bark, or a neighbor's door will slam. But not here. The quiet continued to impose itself.

"I think we should talk about love," said June.

"Love is in the eye of the beholder," said Gene.

"June," said Elsa. "There's a painted goose on the front porch. Do you know where it came from?"

This story could have ended nicely after the wood thrush called from the back of June and Gene's house. But Gertie had been stolen. Stolen from Tommy's front porch. Perhaps that should have been mentioned when Tommy and Elsa first spied Gertie, but Gene interrupted. There wasn't even time for a meaningful glance.

"A little truck came by one day with a hurdy-gurdy playing," said Gene. "He was selling porch geese and garden gnomes."

"Is it possible they were undocumented?" Tommy's hand had begun to ache. It felt better if he held it up but then he was afraid someone would call on him.

"Are you suggesting our goose is hot?"

"We know her. I'm pretty sure I painted her face," Elsa said. "I didn't have the right color for her bill. Is it a bill or a beak?"

"I seriously doubt that," June said.

"It's a mean thing to steal a goose," said Elsa. "I bought outfits for Gertie: Halloween, Christmas, Easter."

"There was only the Easter basket," said June.

"You know, Elsa, I don't think all this red stuff is barbecue sauce. I'm thinking maybe a few stitches might be a good idea."

Gene picked up his plate and started back toward the house. "More gauze, June."

The emergency room wasn't busy, but it was three a.m. before Tommy and his five stiches were cleared for takeoff. There had been some grim remarks about blood alcohol, but Tommy assured the young woman in scrubs that Henry had been sober as a post.

There was a bleached circle on their front porch where Gertie had rested for several years. Elsa sighed. "Your friends stole our porch goose."

"Do you want to press charges?"

Elsa only pursed her lips and blinked at him a few times.

They entered their home together, both listening for the anticipated moment when the door closed solidly behind them.

Names of the Saints

Diving Beetles and Waterbugs

Think of rain, of swimming in the lake, being nibbled by small fish, of the front yard when you were a small child, filling with run off, the water warm and grass underneath, grass between your toes, and the mown detritus floating away, rushing away. It is still raining, but slackening, and the rainbow is double – you run and slide into the water, creating a wake as big as you are. Get up, run, and splash again. After a while you are cold and prune-y. In the lake you jump from a tower with two levels, always from the lower level which is high enough. Sometimes the water comes back through your nose. It is never as much fun as it seems it is going to be. Water Boatman. Eastern Toe-Biter. Also Water Striders. And the little ones, size of teardrops, spinning bumper cars. Whirlagig Beetles. Beneath, clinging to the mossy vegetation, large Diving Beetle, ferocious water bug. And you, you are ferocious, too.

Earwigs and Silverfish

Firebrat. Jumping Bristletail. Silverfish. Silverfish like minnows swimming through the pages of a book, through these pages, but silverfish do not flash, they plough. They are not goldfish, not platinum fish, nor, as in the case of flutes, blackwoodfish. Earwigs do not visit ears, but wigs... A wig of earwigs, gleaming silver, flashing, misbehaving. Wigs do not hide. And how could a bristletail do anything else but jump?

Caterpillars

Wooly Bear. Question Mark. Jars of them, picked and plucked. Pickled and plucked. Stinging hairs, flowing fur, bird fatteners. Tent caterpillar, wads of webs, bagworms, neatly sewn in. Monarch, hornworm, saddleback. Inchworm may I have a dime? Alice's hookah-smoking caterpillar. One pill makes you smaller. If mother wasp does not sit on your back, you'll change into something, never fear. Listen to the music.

Hopperlike

Squash Bug. Alas. Wheel Bug. Stegasaurian grandeur. And the wheel a watch- cog worn like a keel. Green Stink Bug. O slow and green, both bass and treble in my ear, bring on in ink your handsome stink, my dear.

Toad Bugs

Summer sidewalks in the firefly hour. Hold the toad at arm's length for his fat defensive pee. Then everyone feels better. Toad bug. Antennae hidden under the eyes. Like a small pebble that hops.

Beetles

Striped Blister beetle and tumble bug. Golden Net-wing and Fiery Searcher. Patent-leather, Red Turpentine, Elephant Stag. Although the stag is more rhinoceros than elephant. June bugs and May beetles. Like moths, light loving. They will crash into screen doors and windows, careless fliers, blinded by light-lust. Moth lust. (Gypsy Moth, Clothes Moth, Meal Moth, Fairy Moth, Hebrew – what kind of name for a moth is Hebrew?) But this is beetle lust. Bombardier, scarab, dung. Paper clip beetle. Pocket watch beetle. Waterbug-earwig-oriental rat flea-Sergeant Pepper beetle.

Grasshoppers and Crickets

August in the hayloft and the air is half dust, half sun and you are jumping from the piled bales and sliding ten feet or so. Outside, cicadas are ratcheting. Jerusalem Cricket. Mormon Cricket. Turning over boards for their soft black bodies. Feed them to fish, to toads, to turtles. Logs, stones hide worlds. Grasshoppers (American Bird, Green Valley) falling to the bottom of the weed stems, clambering both up and down. Gladiator Katydid. Nebraska Cone-head. Dogday Harvestfly. Digging up from roots. It's time. It's time. Sing and saw. Cow Killer. Giant Lacewing. Texan Snakefly. Giant Stonefly. Snake Doctors. Snake Nurses.

Mites

Velvet Mite. The inside of instrument cases is always velvet. The rich covering of emerging antlers is called velvet. In time, it begins to fall away, shred and hang like Spanish moss. A brand of American cheese is called Velveeta. The cases are closed and no light falls upon the blue or the red velvet. The violin is silent. The flute lonely.

The trumpet is sour brass. The velvet mite is also invisible. Velvet ants are intensely hairy wasps. Females will defend themselves by inflicting a terrible sting or by playing the accordion.

Spiders

Orb Weaver. Black Widow. Brown Recluse. Spider silk is stronger than spider cotton. In Sister Bay, Wisconsin, there is a phone booth from which there is a lovely view of Sister Bay, a fractalic bump in Green Bay. At precisely 6:17 p.m. Central Standard Time, at least 30 spiders descend from their hiding places overhead. They sway and swing, behaving like pendulums, like yo-yos. The person holding a telephone in one hand has the sensation of being under water. The telephone cord is covered with a metal mesh, something like interlocking fish scales such as are found upon alligator gar. This cord is inflexible and would allow the telephone receiver to jerk and sway about if it were not for the vice-like grip that holds it. You are standing in that booth, watching the setting sun glint from the bay, and you are shrinking yourself into the periphery of a pencil, make that a hydrogen atom, as the spiders dance in ever-diminishing concentric circles about you. The telephone in your hand wants to be a water bug, a huge cast bell. You think. Rabid Wolf Spider. Hammock Spider. Violin Spider. You think. The telephone sucks a voice from the disembodied world. Waiting, waiting, then it rings. Wrapped voice waiting. Wandering Spider. Spitting Spider. Spiders have eyes after the manner of gun turrets on battleships. They do not sing in tune. Their webs are sticky and the wind worries them. When spiders die, they do not cease moving because of this habit of wind. Elegant Crab Spider.

Moths and Butterflies

Spring Azure. Green Swallowtail. Red Admiral. Viceroy. Queen. Monarch. Oh, in a world of monarchs, this common creature migrating the length and breadth of the earth – see them covering trees with their fragile fanning. The milkweed plant oozes a white viscous sap as any child can tell. Upon it live a host of creatures which can choose no other home. The monarch caterpillar is like a lovely tangerine, juice fairly bursting behind a bulging skin, a delicious sight as it plows its slow path around the milkweed. It must, however, taste unpleasant. Like a cow on rank grass. I cannot decide whether to try one. In the fall, the white pods grow dry, and shaped like a Gypsy's shoe, split open. Wonderful white parachutes emerge and the seeds fly away, spiders under silk. By this time, the monarchs are floating south. California Dog Face. Cloudless Sulfur. Giant Swallowtail. Songs of the hermit thrush. Silence of the woodpecker. Early Hairstreak. Phoebus. Painted Lady. Resting, the wings are held upright. Moths rest wings flat, horizontal. Butterflies swarm in muddy places, coiled tongues uncoiling. One lights upon my arm, those exquisitely tiny feet clinging, trusting, that coiled proboscis sucking sweat. Wood Nymph. White Peacock. Question Mark. California Dog Face. Lighting on flowers and shit alike. Creatures of the light. Red Admiral. Queen. Sounding like a set for an Irish band. Rattlebox Moth. Alfalfa Looper. Black Witch. On the window glass at night. Whores of the all-night. Spreading their wings shamelessly. Pheromone seekers. Enormous in the pure darkness of night, they shrink to the size of windows when they are touched by light. Hummingbird. And very like hummingbirds they are, flying low as I chase them among the flowers, their wings a blur. With your net you chase them, your breathing, your untied sneakers. Their wings, the grass, their striped bodies, all a blur. Now you watch them on my window, emissaries of the night. O let me in, they cry. (You translate from their bad French.) Let me die in a candle flame. O sweet immolation. Light at the heart of light. Remember us.

PART II

HOUSES

Walter's House

One need not be a Chamber – to be Haunted
    Emily Dickinson

he phone call was from a lawyer who practiced in James' hometown – a man whose name was Walter Eldridge had left him a property in his will. James remembered the lawyer because he had helped to sell his father's house, but Walter Eldridge?

While the lawyer, whose name was Charlie Riley, talked about the property, James tried to remember. There was an old couple named Eldridge who lived across the street. For a number of years, James' father had rented the Eldridge's garage to shelter a series of DeSotos and Chrysler Imperials he bought and sold frequently – all of them huge and adorned with gaudy tail-fins, barely fitting inside the tiny garage.

Mr. Eldridge (James had never heard him called by his first name) owned a fishing pond outside of town. James had fished there several times – once he had spent the night in the cabin. And this was what Eldridge had left to him?

"This isn't a joke, is it? I hardly knew Walter Eldridge."

"Ten acres, a pond, a woodlot, and assorted buildings is no joke. Your father's will was a joke. Leaving me the cobblestone he claimed he tripped over because I wouldn't help him sue the town was a joke. Walter Eldridge's will is the real thing."

"Why me?"

"You're starting to sound like Job," Charlie said. "It's a long story, but Walter has been feuding with his family for years. His wife died the same year your father passed away, and that was the last voice of reason. My advice to you is to get up here and take care of the paperwork, and then we'll see if we can sell it before more trouble starts."

"You mean the rightful heirs?"

"You're the rightful beneficiary. He liked you. He remembered you. Apparently the ability to close a gate goes a long way with Walter. Went a long way. He mentioned it in the will."

James remembered going fishing in the pond. It was a summer after he had gone away to school. There were gates, too. The first one had a big padlock, and then there were others. Had there been livestock? He had a fly rod and he waded around the pond with his right leg in the water so he could clear his back cast. He caught bluegill and rock bass on tiny popping bugs. That one time, Mr. Eldridge had given him the keys to the cabin. He remembered a dream – something about a giant catfish. And he woke up the next morning with his right knee swollen up like a melon. You can't mount a bad knee above your mantelpiece.

Because he was between classes, James told Charlie he had nothing better to do and would drive up the next day. There was a new Holiday Inn just outside the bypass, otherwise, Charlie said, the town hadn't changed at all. James' parents' house looked just the same – it still had the two stained-glass windows the purchaser wouldn't agree to let James take out and preserve. The only difference James noted as he drove past was a Confederate flag in an upstairs window and multiple mailboxes by the door. The house had been made into rental apartments. Once it had been almost grand, but now it had only a postage stamp's worth of yard. James wondered if his mother's tulips still came up.

After that rushed meeting with Charlie (whom James was beginning to think of importantly as his solicitor) – after signing more papers than he had when he closed on his house in Nashville, he decided he might as well see his property. He got lost and had to retrace his route back to town, and get a map from Charlie's secretary. The countryside was rolling with occasional hilltop vistas, more like Virginia than Missouri. Then he found the driveway and the locked gate and was reminded of the little fishing clubs his father belonged to before he gave up chewed-up thumbs and bass slime for golf. James and his father had fished together frequently. There were always gates and padlocks, cattle guards, twisted wire, weeds brushing the bottom of the car, lurching along the ruts.

The keys Charlie gave him were a mix of new copies and old bent originals, carefully marked with masking tape. The gate key was a new copy and James thought it was not going to work, but he was in no hurry, and the padlock finally took pity on him. There had been cattle in this field, but not recently. The pies were old and firm. James closed the gate carefully with some difficulty, pulling it over the grown-up weeds, but not closing the lock. The odds that padlock would work twice in a row were not good. James made a mental note to talk to Charlie about a new padlock.

The next gate was open and the road curved around a dense woodlot. James didn't remember it, but he was keen to get to the lake. In his fishing days, he would get so excited his hands would shake as he assembled his tackle. All this over catching a few little fish. James didn't even like to eat fish. Once he had made a fire and grilled a bass on a pond bank immediately after catching it. It had tasted like mud with fish bones.

A second counter curve of road, more trees and then the grassy shoulder of the earth berm that formed the deep end of the pond. There was a grown-over parking area partially shaded by several thorny locust trees. After James had climbed up to the pond, he could see the cabin on the far side. Was it a pond or a lake? It had probably been created originally to provide water for cattle – there was a rusty trough near the place where he had parked his car. But even in the time when he had visited it in his student days, it was used mostly for fishing and swimming. And the cabin was no shack – it was a small house or cottage, and it was a long walk away. The key marked "cabin" on the keychain did not seem to be a recent duplicate. It was likely to work.

Was it the tableau of the blue water guarded by cattails that reminded him? His knee buckled and almost dropped him – sometimes the knee would hold up – but sometimes it grinded and sometimes it froze. James stood and waited. He was a veteran persuader of bad knees. That was when he noticed the muskrat hole, quite overgrown, but in the line of his next step. Better a fussy knee than a broken leg.

Taking a wide detour around the muskrat's engineering, He made for the cabin, the knee dependable again. He used to keep a travel fly rod in his trunk, but that was another car, he remembered. Still, that blue water was attractive, and not over-fished. No signs of vandalism on the cabin. The windows were intact but there was a particularly robust wasp nest suspended from the roof at the corner of the porch. Make a note for Charlie. Wasp stings don't encourage buyers.

The porch was solid underfoot – not yet undermined by muskrats and woodchucks. The key could easily be persuaded to turn the old loose lock mechanism.

First a waft of wood ashes, an entirely pleasant association with cabins and fireplaces. Then a crash and a terrible racket from the back of the cabin, jolting James from his reverie. But, pounding heart or not, he was the landlord, and that grizzly bear was his to scold if he so chose. He cast about for a weapon. The hat rack beside the door would have to do. It was so ridiculous, he felt calmer. He stalked through the front room, past the handsome stone fireplace. Some of the stones had fossils – Permian, Devonian? Then the kitchen. A little musty smelling, but empty. A door to a porch or a mudroom presented the last possible refuge for the intruder. James listened carefully. Apart from his heart, he could hear nothing. He set down the hat rack and put his hand on the doorknob. Turned it. Pulled gently. Nothing. Idiot. The door swings outward. Hat rack back in hand he pushed the door, and it swung slowly open. Here was a laundry room, perhaps once a porch, now enclosed with cheerful windows all around. The door to the outside stood open. Then James noticed a shelf behind the washer and dryer had come down on one side, dumping its contents of laundry detergent and various cleaning aids. Outside there was no path – just a half cord of firewood under a shed roof. The hillside was covered in weeds, Queen Ann's lace, torchwood, wild mustard, and it was all rocking in a freshening breeze. Clouds had humped up. James could not see it but he knew the pond would be steely and rough now, no longer blue. He saw no person, no bear, no reason why there would have been a lighted candle in a sconce opposite the washer and dryer. As he watched, the wind blew it out. Was he hallucinating? He touched the wax at its base. It was hot.

Back inside, he took the time to notice the furniture – a round oak table. A few sturdy chairs. An old Morris chair with upholstered cushions that felt like horsehair when he sat in it. It groaned, but it might have been a groan of welcome. James sat and rested his arms on the wide flat arms of the Morris chair. There were several bookshelves. After dusting he could check them out more carefully, but he saw Hemingway stories. Then Henry James. *The Golden Bowl. The Turn of the Screw.* Then Kraft-Ebbing: *Psychopathia Sexualis.* A very old book. From the library of Dr. Alfred Jones, 1936. James' grandfather had been a country doctor in a neighboring town. He couldn't imagine how one of his books could find its way to this place. James had last seen it in the front hall bookcase of the house with the two stained glass windows. When his mother realized James the schoolboy was reading them, she packed them up and stored them in the attic.

Another crash. And loud. But this was thunder. A summer shower had come visiting. James stood on the front porch and watched the lines of wind and rain drawing nests on the pond and then erasing them. Another lightning flash and closely following peal of thunder sent him back into the house. He automatically raked the light switch by the door. Lights came on. A rather fancy ceiling light with three bulbs made him think momentarily of a jester. The ceiling was low. There by the kitchen door – a steep staircase. He did not recall visiting the upper story on his previous visit. He had slept on a divan that had unfortunately been visited by cats. Perhaps that strange dream was the result of the odor of feline urine.

In the kitchen James found the usual suspects, secondhand yard sale pots and pans, dishes and the like. He rinsed a glass with water that came out clear if reluctantly. A well? It tasted all right. There was no bathroom on the ground floor. What was upstairs, anyway?

The stairs were steep and narrow. James fancied he had boarded a pirate ship. At the top of the stairs, three doors, the one directly in front was the bathroom. He used it. The toilet was functional. He turned back to the hallway. The other doors led to a front bedroom and a back bedroom.

James opened the door to the front bedroom. There was an empty room, carpeted, but with no furniture. The ceiling was shaped by the pitch of the roof. As he stood there, the overhead light came on, startling him, then after a brief moment, it went off. The wall switch had no effect on it. Make a note to have Charlie call an electrician. One room to go, then. Should he knock? Perhaps it would have mattered. The storm was moving away, its thunder pleasantly faint in the distance. James opened the door.

Perhaps a dozen lit candles were arranged on a dresser and chest of drawers. They seemed to draw up the gloom of the room rather than to light it. There was a small bed covered in sheets but no apparent bedspread. Underfoot, the same carpet as the front room but it was covered with throw rugs, oval and rectangular. And a rocking chair rocking lightly, but empty. Its occupant was not in the room as far as James could see. The closet door stood open showing its bare and spare insides – a few bent metal hangers.

Still holding on the doorknob, he took a step further into the gloom. There was something on the bed. It was some kind of arrangement. The skull of some kind of small animal, perhaps a dog, something with prominent incisors. A stack of dried weeds. A water glass with what appeared to be tadpoles swimming briskly in it. When something moved in the weeds, he had had enough. He did not break his neck descending the stairs because he was able to grab hold of the banister. He did not lock the door behind him. It had been a salamander or the flaring of a gill. Some animal or part of an animal out of place. Terribly out of place. When he got to the car, his pants were soaked to the knees from the wet undergrowth. His shoes were muddy. He had not had much to eat that morning, but that he left on the weedy gravel.

As he bounced back to the locked gate and the gravel road which would lead him to the two-lane blacktop and on to the little town and to his lawyer's quaint little office, glass-fronted, facing the courthouse on the town square, he began reasoning with himself.

Someone in the family, then, cheated out of this inheritance, had decided to play a little trick. Well, a medium sized trick – but in the category of mischief. Someone who had taken a book full of bizarre case histories from the white house with two stained glass windows he used to live in. If he were not tired from driving 400 miles, he probably could have appreciated the humor of it at the time.

But those candles could start a fire. And trespassing is trespassing. His hypothesis was reasonable. The alternative was a bloody spook of some sort who was warming up to suck the life out of him by causing his heart to explode. That would make a good story. But finding the prankster would be a good one, too. One he could tell with a glass of Jack Daniels in his hand, cold beads of moisture, swirling ice cubes. Even without a story, he could use that drink. Maybe Charlie would still be in his office.

The storm had been through town, too. There were standing puddles on the courthouse lawn. The office door was locked but Charlie saw him standing there and let him in. In that moment, it occurred to James that Charlie did not look like a lawyer. Perhaps there was a suit jacket or a blazer hanging in his closet, but James had never seen it. Charlie's hair was thinning and his manner was furtive, rather than small-town-hearty. He gave James a hard look, spun on his heel and headed toward the back of the office.

"Nobody home but me. You look like you could use a drink."

He poured out something brown. No ice. That's what comes of small town life, James thought.

"The other guy look worse than you?"

"I wish I knew," James said and he drank the brown stuff. Wild turkey or wild boar or feral cat. He swallowed too much and coughed. So much for manly appearances.

James told Charlie there were lighted candles in the cabin and that he had gotten caught in the rain, and threw in a muskrat hole because it was more plausible than haunted tadpoles.

"You're smiling," James pointed out as Charlie poured him a few more fingers.

"Your father and Walter didn't get on too well toward the end,"

Charlie said. He was beginning to look hearty after all.

James waited.

"It started with the garage. You want to hear this?"

James didn't, but he nodded affirmatively.

Charlie sighed. "Walter's daughter used to come over and clean and cook. Your father would drop in and chat."

James nodded again. His father would trip a stranger just to strike up a conversation. And he was a dirty old man.

"Walter didn't like it. There were words. Some shoving. Hey, it's a small town. Besides, Walter told me."

"Then why did he leave that property to me?"

"I think his daughter took up for your father. Maybe it was something else. Walter didn't like the guy she was hanging out with – he was real trouble. But you don't need to hear that story.

Charlie got up and fiddled with some books on the shelves behind his desk.

With his back turned he said something James almost had to ask him to repeat, but then it came to him. "What do you want to do?"

"I'd like to go back there with a witness. Maybe a deputy."

"Well, that's the advice I ought to give you."

He turned around. "But I really ought to see that place before we send some innocent real estate agent to her candle-lit doom. Want to go now? You couldn't get any muddier."

I could, James thought. But he had a change of clothes back at the motel. Charlie pulled something that looked like a tan safari jacket out of his closet. He dressed like a news anchor.

"Am I paying for this?" James couldn't help himself.

"This one's on the house. Just seeing you at the door made my day."

On the way back to his old fishing hole James asked Charlie about the Eldridge children.

"There's Sally. She was closest to her father – and the one your father found so charming. She was living with a guy who got busted for a meth lab. She went west."

"You sure?"

"It's a small town."

"Earl's been dead almost ten years. Bridge abutment. Then there's Duane."

"Duane."

"He's the youngest. Farms. No tweaker. But he might grow a little marijuana."

"Where does he farm?"

"Around here. Want to open that gate?" He grinned. "Did you stop to lock it?"

"It was raining." James hopped out and held open the gate so Charlie could drive his bright red Silverado past him a little farther than necessary. James mounted up after taking some extra time fiddling with the gate chain to reassert the importance of his task.

"My father used to let me ride on the fender when I opened gates."

"It's a wonder he didn't run you over."

"Yet here I am."

Charlie pulled into the parking area and turned around, making a show of the spinning steering wheel which he had fitted with a professional-looking spinner knob.

"Now the ghosts know we're here," James said and immediately felt foolish.

Charlie grunted something James decided not to ask him to repeat. The two men labored up to the cabin in silence.

"Those wasps must go," James said, pointing.

"Why don't you make a list and I'll see to it." Charlie was walking the perimeter of the cabin, looking, James realized, for footprints.

"The noise came from this back room," James said when they got to the lean-to and firewood. Charlie tried the back door and it proved to be locked.

"We don't have a key for this door. Add that to the list."

"I don't have a list."

"Then remember it."

There were no footprints but the tall weeds were beaten down. The cabin had been built on a hillside and it got steep after a few yards.

'You could climb up there and look down on the roof," Charlie said, thoughtfully.

"You could also climb up there, slip, and break your neck."

"That's true." Charlie examined a bent weed and was rewarded by a nest of cockleburs clinging to the arm of his jacket.

"We have keys to the front door," James reminded him.

"So we do." He sighed, and led the way through the still-wet weeds back to the front door, still peeling burrs from the sleeve of his safari jacket. James could hear a red-winged blackbird from the pond. They built their nests in the cattails and would harass anyone who got too close. It was late afternoon, but the sky had cleared. The world smelled like wet dirt and drying weeds. The porch smelled like mildew.

Without hesitating, Charlie thrust the key into the lock and opened the door.

"Look at this," he said.

And when James had followed him in the door, he saw an empty room. Had his words been clipped? James walked briskly through the room, through the kitchen, opened the door to the back mudroom / laundry room. Nothing. There was no candle in the sconce. Back to the fireplace.

"Hey Charlie." James was aware of the sound of his voice in the empty room. There was a slight echo. Beyond that, his voice, if it showed anything, betrayed slight irritation. It would not do to take the hat rack up those steep stairs. There were knives in the kitchen, but James wasn't comfortable with knives. Why did he need a weapon, anyway? He climbed the steps then with nothing but a strangling grip on the banister.

Bathroom: door open. Empty. Front bedroom: He opened the door. Nothing. The same lack of furnishings. The overhead light still didn't work. Back bedroom: He opened the door.

"Charlie?"

It was dark. No lit candles. There was a heavy curtain hanging over the window. James switched on the ceiling light. No one in the room. No candles on the dresser or the chest of drawers. No wax on the dresser. The chest was clean. The closet door was open. The bed was covered with an old chenille spread – a faded white or gray. Once it had been some color or other. No tadpoles in a jar, no creeping disgusting witch messages. The room was clean. The room was empty.

"Dammit, Charlie!" James pulled the curtain away from the window too forcefully and the curtain rod came down. The pond had grown quite calm – it was probably a good time for fishing. The room, now lit, seemed innocuous, if a little lonely. Nothing under the bed.

James heard the Silverado starting up. This time his feet stayed on the stairs.

Out the front door. From the porch he could see a red truck pulling out of the parking area and driving away – it didn't seem in any haste.

His cell phone? It was in his car. Why would he need a phone if he was riding in a big red truck with his solicitor? A blackbird trilled from the cattails.

In the living room again. He looked around himself. What was he missing? Behind the Morris chair there was a door. No handle, but a lock. This house had a basement. He moved the chair, and there on the floor were the keys, the keys he had handed over to Charlie. There were a half dozen keys but only two were marked: gate and cabin.

"Hey Charlie. Are you down there?" Loud enough, he thought. The first unmarked key did not work. The second was accepted but would not turn. The third turned the entire lock. He left the key in the lock and gathered up that most useless of all self-defense weapons from the fireplace, a poker. The key was stuck. As he pulled to get it out, the door came open.

No light, of course. And these stairs were even steeper than the ones to the second story. He had seen a flashlight in the kitchen, on a shelf over the stove.

Flashlight in one hand, poker in the other, he descended the basements stairs which had no railing or banister anyway. At the bottom he cast the light around, revealing a furnace and water heater. The floor was firm concrete and a ground-level window let in a little weed-screened light.

"Charlie?"

James moved past the furnace and there found a hanging bulb with a pull string. This was the cleanest basement he had seen in a long time. And dry. Why do we say dry as a bone? Finally, in the far corner, a workbench, and strewn across it, fishing tackle, including a rather study spinning rod and reel. James picked out a few items, thought about turning off the light, decided against it, then climbed the steep stairs. He managed to get the keys out of the lock and closed the door. He pushed the chair back in place and made one more complete tour of the cabin. It was a nice little house when it wasn't haunted.

   The cattails had made about half of the pond difficult to approach. If you hooked a fish in the open water, you'd have to steer it through those dense water weeds. James had lost many a fish in cattails. You can also soak them in kerosene and they make a neat torch (if you're fourteen). James found an open spot where perhaps a neighbor boy had sat with cane pole and worms, if young people did such things anymore. He had brought a small tackle box and several shallow-diving lures, the kind that vibrate like the last spin cycle of a washing machine. If Charlie was going to abandon him and drive back to town – if the entire Blair Witch Project was going to decamp and move to greener silos, he was going to catch a few fish. And he did. Several small bass and one large enough to leap clear of the surface and spit that piece of plastic with its attendant swarm of hooks directly at his eye. James stepped back, causing him to miss. He should have laughed, but he began to frown. He reeled in the slack line, removed the lure, and fumbled through the batch of lures he had brought from the basement. There was one large spoon, the hooks so sharp, they drew a drop of blood while he was attaching it. James made a few more desultory casts, mainly to the middle of the pond, where even a poor fisherman knows there are few fish. Perhaps, he thought, ghosts are like fish, essentially shy of the living. Now they must be in hiding. James cast the spoon a last time toward the middle of the pond and let it sink. He laid down the rod. There was a time when he would have smoked a cigarette. This time he walked along the bank until a scolding red winged blackbird brought him up short.

Abandoning the pond, he spent the next hour wandering around the estate, his estate, following paths and faint tracks, peering in windows of outbuildings, trying keys in locks. He was looking for another fish big enough to spit hardware at him, but he found nothing. He scared a blacksnake and the blacksnake scared him even while he was making his escape. Maybe Charlie remembered something critical and had to rush back to town. Any minute and he would be explaining that he rarely threw on his cloak of invisibility, and he would be offering more plausible excuses than James at this moment could imagine.

He had fish slime on his hands and his thumb was abraded from the Velcro-like teeth of the fish's mouths. The cabin's screen door creaked as he let himself in. The Morris chair creaked in kind. James watched the light change as clouds passed overhead.

"No." He stood up so quickly the back cushion of the chair fell onto its seat. His knee buckled, but he grabbed the chair arm and waited it out. Then James walked out the door, swatting absently at several wasps circling near the porch. On the pond bank, his rod and reel lay abandoned, next to the small rusty tackle box he had brought up from the basement.

He picked up the rod and reeled in the slack line. The spoon had snagged on something on the pond's bottom. James hauled back cautiously. The snag was firm. Perhaps an old tree trunk. James hauled again. It began to give. Slowly he heaved and reeled, heaved and reeled. The red winged blackbird chirred from the other side. A small bullfrog plunked its banjo. His feet sank into watery mud. With the last heave, something rose into view. James let it sink back, his breathing shallow and rapid. Then he heaved another time. The safari jacket came clearly into view. It rolled and an arm rose up out of the water as it turned. As if in greeting.

The Station

The funeral had been ordinary enough – except for the fact I was inside the church I had grown up within – and then let a good fifty years pass before this return. I had known the deceased when I was a child, a friendly fellow who worked for my father in his grocery store, and then curiously stayed friends with him until his death. Why had I made a seven-hour drive to attend a stranger's funeral? My wife was in Florida tending to her ninety-year-old mother. Maybe it was adventure. Maybe I wanted to look over the town. John was survived by his wife – I observed she was an old woman. I remembered her as a high school girl, one who never spoke to me, an underclassman. I did not speak to her, or anyone else. Since I did not recognize anybody, I could be reasonably certain nobody would recognize me.

I had spent the morning driving around. I saw the Hockaday House, a highpoint for me back in the day – the town's only real mansion. But I couldn't get close – the grounds were cordoned off for some kind of reconstruction or repair. I found, with some difficulty, the little road, gravel when I first knew it, where I spent my elementary years. The huge field I had enjoyed walking through on the way to school was a maze of streets and little houses, some quaint, and some well on the way to seedy. The school was unchanged, but I did not linger. There is a thin line between lingering and lurking.

The church was Methodist and the people in it were Methodists and I learned that John had returned to it after he retired from some kind of esoteric government job in Washington, D.C. Methodists are not as excitable as Baptists nor as uppity as Presbyterians. Apparently John's favorite song was *Jesu Joy of Man's Desiring*. I did not view the body – yes, I am squeamish. And I had a strong feeling my delicious anonymity might be compromised. John wouldn't have minded. I did have fleeting thoughts about the corpse jolting upright and spitting salt water, but we were a good thousand miles from salt water and John seemed far too relaxed.

I knew the buffet in the church basement for family and friends would be excellent – I wavered as the minister droned on. A good life is a boring life, he seemed to say, and I realized I would have to supply like details related to mine own.

No, I would slip away and begin my journey home. I had parked a block away from the church within sight of the big white house where I spent my high school years. I sold it when my father died and hoped to keep the stained glass window that colored the light in my bedroom, but the purchaser wanted that window. And there had been little interest in the house because, among other deficiencies, it had no yard. I counted six mailboxes and wondered who got the window.

It would be dark soon, so I prepared to make my way back toward the Interstate – but I couldn't help a quick detour to my old high school where I had admired John's wife from afar. It was now a middle school but it seemed to know me, and was not apologetic about appearing in my dreams with endless gleaming corridors and labyrinthine stairways. It was so small now.

I heard thunder. This was the place I gazed out the window during Mr. Tice's algebra class. Where was the tree I used to watch? More thunder. A brick building near the road at the edge of town. Bell Press the large sign said. I thought for years it was a place where bells were made. But it was a printing press.

The sky darkened; the world around me darkened. A large raindrop splatted on the windshield. Then I drove into a curtain of falling water. I was on a state road angling toward the interstate, an old shortcut. I slowed and the rain became heavier – if I could get to the interstate, perhaps I could follow a truck – it was my good luck there was no traffic on this road.

Then the rain stopped, but it was as dark as the inside of a dog. I rounded the access ramp in the midst of a sopping field – animals were hiding out there, birds and rabbits. Perhaps an old box turtle I had known for a time when I was a boy. Why not? They live long.

Then I headed east on a fairly deserted highway, and the heavens opened again. This time it was The Red Sea and I was not doing any parting. Hail and small fish flashed in my squinting vision. I crept along the right lane, hoping for an exit. I thought I knew where I was. When I found it, I excused myself, wishing the water gods well. Now I was creeping along the old East / West highway, the one replaced by the Interstate. There used to be restaurants and motels. Now there was nothing. My grandmother had run a general store and gas station only a few miles from where I imagined I was driving and her husband farmed. She had divorced my grandfather long before I was born. No one would tell me that story. The rain was intent on spawning Noah's flood. I found a driveway and something like a parking lot. I would wait it out. I turned on the radio. Nothing. There is never nothing on the radio. It had been a long day, a long two days. I fell asleep and when I woke a few hours later, the rain was less furious but steady and determined. If the state police found me sleeping, they could lead me to a dry place. I resolved to spend the rest of the night in place. No more driving. I couldn't see in the dark.

Then morning. Some gray light in the car with me, sharing space with my aches and pains. It had been a dreamless sleep. No. There had been a sound. Sounds. Something distant and then slowly approaching, pitch rising, then a swirl of passing and dimuendo. Until it was gone. Trucks passing. A lonely sound. I remembered summers staying with my grandmother, trying to get to sleep in the summer heat. This was long before I or anyone I knew had any notion of air conditioning. A single truck in the night. The highway was close to the front of the store. There were gas pumps and a canopy. A big window to look out. "There's a car out front," my grandmother would call.

My windows were fogged over, but there was no more rain. Maybe I had been hearing trucks from the Interstate, out of sight but surely not that far away. I opened the door and stepped outside. My legs ached. My back felt bent like a paper clip. I was parked by a maple tree, several maple trees and there was a county road, arrow-straight, perpendicular to the old highway, bounding a wheat field. I relieved myself in the maple grove. When I was done there was still the sound of water. Two hundred yards to the west, the direction from which I had come, the road was flooded. A stream had topped its banks. And to the east the highway would end. I remembered that much. I was here for a longer stay than I had planned.

There was a building, a filling station with old pumps. One was the kind you pump by hand and then gravity feeds it into the car, an antique. There was a Sinclair Oil sign with its handsome dinosaur. There were no vehicles – the place was deserted. A screen door in front and two large windows, one on either side. You couldn't see inside. Deserted, desolate. Attached to the rear of the square central shape, a garage with a large door in the side, partially raised, showing a horizontal black shadow. Behind it a large garden and an old orchard. The trees seemed to be dead. There would be a pond beyond the orchard, a corncrib and a hog pen. This was the image of my grandmother's place. She and Henry sold it and moved into town, into a little house I didn't think to look for on a street called Bluff Street because there were real bluffs on the other side of the creek that bounded their backyard. This was the place they sold – they called it *the station*. And it had burned down. I saw it myself. There was nothing but a house trailer on the spot where it had stood. And that trailer had burned down. Nothing remained. Just a gravel road that arrowed south, that gave the farmers a way to get out of their miles of soy beans, corn, and wheat.

Of course, this wasn't the station, but it looked like it. I had spent summers feeding the hogs, weeding the garden, even driving a tractor, a little Ford tractor which seemed enormous to me. My parents wanted me away for some reason. I hadn't thought about it at the time. I was homesick. My grandmother was a busy woman. I should learn to be a busy child.

I walked around to the front, under the canopy. Through the right window I could see a little – no appliances, a kitchen table, linoleum or something like it on the floor. Nobody in the kitchen. I could see nothing through the left window – it had been painted on the inside. I could see the brush marks in the paint. The screen door would open but the door behind it was locked. It rattled when I tried it. I knocked, then knocked again louder. Nothing. To the west, I could hear the flooded roadway gurgling.

I walked back around the building toward the garage door. There was a wheat field to the east behind me and sunrise was producing long shadows. Another maple tree, branching low, about waist high. The first tree I ever climbed was a maple – very like this one. It must be dead. I climbed all the way to the top, so far up I could not see the ground for the leaves. When my grandmother called me, I didn't answer. I was in another world.

The garage door was very large – large enough for a small truck. I tried to see if I could raise it, but it was locked in place.

At this point I walked back to my car – there was a water bottle in the trunk – a drink of water to settle my thinking. Where was I? No traffic on the roadway. No sounds from the direction of the interstate. I decided I would look around inside the building. I went back to the garage door, knelt down, and, trying to keep my rear end off the ground, worked myself under the door.

Inside it was dark save for a high window on the far side of this very large space. I heard the spark of a sparrow from the exposed rafters I could see as shadows above. The smell was of dust and oil – about equal. By the side of the door, illuminated by the light coming in under it, was an old welding machine. A welding mask hung on the wall beside it.

There should be a chain winch hanging from the rafters above me, about 15 or 20 feet inside. I could see something above me, just where I remembered it. My eyes were beginning to adjust to the gloom.

The floor was concrete, blotched with a mix of oil stains and shadows. Across it and to my left I should find a hallway passage to the front room, in which I expected to find a counter on two walls and a coal stove converted to kerosene. Perhaps there would be rocking chairs.

Entering the passage, I walked into a spider web – not likely populated but I brushed it off as if it were swarming with wiggly creatures. To my right a closed door. If it weren't so dark, I might see *Gents* painted in a rough freehand. Then in front of me, another closed door. I turned the knob and it opened.

This was once a general store with shelves and glass counters, an old mechanical cash register. I had been trusted to use it. The thing was big as a safe. We sold flour, dry beans, chewing tobacco. There was a case of soda pop. One time an old black man came in and asked for something. He might have been driving a mule hitched to a wagon. I couldn't understand what he said. I asked him again and couldn't understand. Perhaps he had no teeth. I could see him growing (I thought) angry, but it must have been humiliation. I called my grandmother. I had failed a customer. It was Picnic Twist he wanted – chewing tobacco.

The room was empty. No stove or rocking chairs. No counters, but there were shelves on the walls. There was more light coming from the front, even from the painted window. The concrete floor had seams and a large crack, diagonal. I remembered staring at that crack while the adults in their rocking chairs droned on. I sat on a counter stool with bent metal legs.

It was an old abandoned building, too rundown to be of any use. It was supposed to have burned down. I remembered one time driving on the access road to have a look at it, years before. There was nothing, just a crossroads. No maple trees, no orchard, alive or dead. No pond, no corncrib (where I had set live traps for mice, but caught instead, kittens). Maybe I had been in the wrong place.

Here, in the building I remembered, or thought I remembered, I finished my tour.

"Here is the stairway," I said to myself. I might as well be tour guide. The ghosts might not remember me. "Unheated. Climbing it, I saw my breath for the first time. I thought I was on fire. Really. I was five years old." My voice echoed unpleasantly.

At the top of the stairs another hallway with rooms on either side. The first door on the left, my grandmother and Henry, my step grandfather. I did not call him Henry. I didn't call him anything. I was afraid of him. In those days, I never looked in that room. Now, I looked at the door, touched the knob, then thought better of it.

The next door across the hall was open. There was no furniture inside it. I remembered curtains. A bed, of course. I had shared a bed in this room with my cousin Larry who was older than me by several years. He told me he walked in his sleep. That he sometimes dreamed he was fighting. I walked across the room noticing vague marks on the dusty floor. The window looked out on the side of the house where I had often been warned away from the well. A dangerous place for a child. Never stand on the concrete surface.

Below me, the well. And a man standing there, motionless. I stepped back from the window. Now I was the ghost. That night with my cousin, I took my pillow and slept in the corner.

At best, I was trespassing. At worst, I didn't want to think. I made my way down the stairs briskly. In the general store, I realized I might have a choice. The front door might open from the inside. There was, in fact, a deadbolt I could open. I let myself out. Closing the door, I looked around me. I could see my car but no other. Taking a deep breath, I made my way around the building to have a look at my visitor at the well. There was plenty of light now, and birds were singing. I heard a meadowlark from the field across highway. When I reached the well, there was nobody there. All the way around the building then. The garage was long, almost reaching the orchard. Nobody standing by the garage. I realized I used to dream about that garage. I had the dream many times when I was an adolescent. The garage was larger on the inside than on the outside. It went on forever and I wandered through it. I was searching for something – something that has gotten lost in memory. And now I was searching for somebody. It was weedy behind the garage. I plowed through a clump of mint, getting myself wetter than I intended.

Around the garage and back toward the highway. There had been a large garden on this side. This was where Henry let me drive the tractor. I think we were tilling.

No person. He had been standing on the well cover, turned away from me, wearing a dark coat. Something long that hung to his knees. A hat. Did he wear a hat? Maybe it was something like a watch cap. Could he have been Henry? I didn't see his face. Back under the canopy, I heard the gurgling of a mourning dove. There was a nest near the top of a support pillar. I could see my car again. Around to the well one more time. Looking for footprints, I noticed something. The garage door. The door that had been stuck, that I had crawled under. The garage door was completely closed.

In the dream I had found a passage that was supported by those high rafters where the sparrows sparked. I was searching for something I wasn't sure of. But it comes back, little by little. One time, waking, I thought it was a blue stone. Another time, a blue flower. Always I would meet a crone seated in a rocking chair. "Where is it?" I would ask. And always she would not speak. Perhaps she was dead. And then I forgot the dream.

Now I was alone and hungry. Perhaps not alone. Someone might have entered the building in the same manner I used. Someone who was able to close the garage door. I had forgotten my cell phone – I almost never carry it, anyway.

Thinking about the real world, I returned to my car. I remembered the old highway coming to a dead end. But my memory was wrong about this place. When I turned the key, I heard a soft click, then nothing. The way things were going, this was not much of a surprise. Perhaps I could go back to sleep and wake up in a better place. A better place. Poor choice of words.

Had there been anything on those shelves – canned goods, perhaps? I had maybe one and a half bottles of water. Then I heard a sound. Unmistakable. The squeak and slam of a screen door. That got me out of my car and striding toward the canopy. A hungry man is a brave man. But there was nobody under the canopy. The screen door opened with an all too familiar complaint. But the front door which I had left unlocked, not having a key, was locked. Who had locked the door and slammed the screen door? Had I really seen somebody standing on the well?

I remembered there was a farmhouse about a half mile back on the gravel road. There was a pond and I used to take the dogs with me and go fishing. Wherever I was, there might be a farmhouse. Somebody owned that wheat field. So I began walking. I'd leave my ghost to his doors, screen and garage. There had been a dream about this road, too. I was being pursued. Childhood for me had involved a lot of escaping, some of it literal. Bullies were a way of life. They took your lunch money, broke a tooth or two for you on the basketball court. John was not a bully, nor was his wife. There were some good guys. Who was chasing me in the dream? I couldn't remember – I was running fast. Why bother to dream about running fast when you could do it any day in waking life? Well, it was fun – might as well dream it, too. In real life, seventh grade, I ran through at least four squares of wet cement being chased by a half dozen kids. They got caught, standing in wet cement. I ran on. No dream that.

I decided to jog on the gravel road – hardly faster than walking, but a livelier feeling. Wheat field to my right, soybeans to my left. And along the roadside, some handsome thistles, medieval in their armament.

A crossroads. Turn right and the farmhouse would be on the left. And nothing. Maybe a foundation. The farmer moved to the city. And to my right there was a pond, out of sight. I could hear red-winged blackbirds – they nest in cattails. So maybe this was the old place, but what I really needed was a pay phone. Or a pickup truck like this red one approaching.

* * *

Only a few steps brought me to the intersection of southbound gravel county road and (what to call it?) fragmentary, undulating, recently flooded, but apparently accessible east / west US route 40 or 440 (for a good tuning note) or 251 (for a good progression to improvise on). They only involved my introducing myself to an elderly gentleman farmer who, like me, did not have a phone, but there was a land line at home only a few miles away and a daughter making a grocery visit who did indeed have a cell phone and persuaded me to have a plate of fried country ham and eggs and two cups of coffee chatting with Mr. Phil about, of all things, fishing. There were some big fish in that pond whose blackbirds I had heard from a distance and they were most sportingly caught with a fly rod and popping bugs. But because gentleman farmers have commitments, eggs to lay, and worms to scratch, I soon found myself alone again, waiting for AAA.

What else? There was no structure on that corner. My little Corolla was parked next to a very dead and leafless tree that might once have been a maple. There was no general store, no garage, no canopy with antique gas pumps. Furthermore, there was no mobile home (once rumored to have replaced the original structure). There was not much of anything, including a character with a long coat. After all, it was early summer.

I walked around, after assuring myself my car still would not start. The flood waters to the west had abated, and there still was a mourning dove somewhere to the west. I remembered my grandmother called them rain crows. If you heard that soft call, you were going to see some rain. It is a strange sound – something about it seems farther away than it really is. Or maybe nearer.

I did find what had once been a cistern or a well. And on the concrete cap, I found a small blue stone, oblong, about the size of a cigarette lighter. It was the sort of thing I'd have kept in a cigar box when I was a child, along with other treasures. I picked it up, felt its weight, then I threw it as far as I could, over the gravel road and into the wheat field. It was a good long throw.

Encounter

There's a great deal to be said for routine. If the clock's face were blank, there would be no hours. And hours are porpoises that will swim away and leave the best of days empty. My routine then, now that I've retired from teaching: In the morning I walk with the dog. Then I write. The projects come and go. Nearly always a poem. Sometimes a story like this. A trip to the grocery story with the dog who waits in the car, nose to the cracked window, patient, reading the smells from the creek not far away. And in the store, a cast of characters, the old woman with thinning hair, almost every day. Sometimes a row of folding chairs set up for the old folks who come in their bus, sitting primly or prowling about like chickens. And me moving among them with my list – bread and milk. Something like cod from the fish counter if it is already set out and I don't have to beg for clerk's attention. He is a harsh young man, a proud man. He never seems to notice me. He thinks I should have something better to do than shop in a grocery store. Then with my fish and small red potatoes, I find the dog not really waiting for me – she is breathing in the world of that creek. I've been there, too. Years ago I waded it and caught crayfish, even small fish. The fish hide under rocks, turn themselves on their sides to fit and hide.

I drive behind the loading docks, shutting the dog's window to the creek, and home we go, numbers on a clock face. Then the dog and I walk again, a block or two – the neighborhood has sidewalks. The neighbors don't seem to know us – never a wave (hardly anybody has a hat to tip, and the ones who do have never done it in their lives.) We don't stop to talk. After lunch (a sandwich, or a bowl of soup), more writing, perhaps some music. The scales go slower now. The dog will often sing along. It no longer seems ridiculous. Then another walk – in the winter months the dark will come directly out of the clouds above us. Squirrels scrabble in the alleys, running along the tops of fences as we pass. Then more music. Tunes have names like *The Stone in the Field, Ah Surely, I'm Waiting for You*. The dog will sleep or lunge at the door at another dog passing. Some may pass freely. Others are anathema. The mysteries of dogs. There, I've given you my routine – day follows day. The sun or lack of it provides a figured bass.

One day, then, this happened. I was lost in thought, following the dog down an alley. The dog, sniffing, casting about as if blown by the wind, startled. I heard it at the same time, gravel, a single piece of it, spitting under a tire. I moved to the side of the alley without looking, someone's backyard, a winter bed of iris, carefully tied off. The car began to pass us, slowed, then stopped. The reflection of the sky in the window yielded to the face of a young woman, a girl, as the window lowered. I did not recognize her but she seemed to know me.

"What's your dog's name? I've forgotten," she said.

Where does she live? Have I seen her before?

"Her name is Charlotte," I said. Hearing her name, the dog began to wag her tail widely and made a little spin under her leash, a trick she learned when she was a puppy.

The girl laughed. "How did you teach her to do that?"

"I didn't teach her. The trick came with the dog. She does it for the people she likes."

"Yes, I like her. And I like you."

I didn't know what to say. She looked to be…what…seventeen? She couldn't be younger than that and driving a car. Seconds were piling up. I tried something I imagined from my place behind it to be a benign expression. The dog's tail slowed its wagging.

She gave me a beatific smile. "And you like me."

"Of course," I said. I would grandfather this to its very end.

"That's so very nice," she said and smiled enough to start up the dog's tail and then another one to me.

More seconds piling up. "I'll look for you," she said, and gravel began to spit as the car rolled by.

"I'm waiting for you." That's a song I've heard the fiddler Michael Coleman play.

Funny such a young girl would make me think of an old song. She was quite pretty. Her car pulled into a backyard and a high fence gate rolled shut behind it. I realized there was a large puddle beside the iris patch and I was standing in it. But not the dog.

The dog gave me an especially patient look – one that included in its context the fact that I never show her that kind of forbearance when she is sniffing at an interesting corner.

"Sorry, pup," I said, almost wishing there was somebody to hear me having a harmless conversation with my dog.

Maybe she thought I was somebody else, I thought as we made our way home. Somebody else who looks like me and walks a white poodle.

That was the first time. The next day we were walking in the same alley. I like to walk in alleys in this neighborhood. The backyards are quiet, and there are little outbuildings, some of them quite ramshackle, that I can admire at my leisure. I think of them as urban ruins.

We heard a car behind us and it was the same girl, this time waving vigorously. She slowed and the window lowered. Curtains rise and windows lower.

"Make Charlotte do that trick." she insisted.

"You'll have to talk to her – she won't do it for me."

"Charlotte. Charlotte. Hello, Charlotte."

Charlotte, bless her heart, did her do-si-do with considerable enthusiasm. I was proud of my talented dog.

Then we stood there waiting for our lines. I have never had a gift for small talk, if there is such a thing as a gift. I knew a girl once very like this one.

"Oh, well," she said, and drove on down the alley, disappearing into the same gateway which had closed by the time we reached it. If it had not dried up overnight, I would have been standing in the same puddle.

Several days went by and we did not see her. But I saw her from my front porch perhaps a week later. She was putting a violin case in the back of an expensive SUV. I suppose I notice more about cars when they are at a distance. I sped up my pace, but young people are only slow when they want to be – her car pulled away before we got close enough to see. I made a note of the house she came out of. Did it belong to the sliding gate in the alley? It did. If the mystery girl appeared again, I would ask her about the violin.

Then, perhaps a week later, Charlotte and I were walking along the street side of the house I had made careful note of. A middle-aged woman was tending a batch of pansies in her front yard. Charlotte had decided to pick up a fallen dead branch a little too large to carry and was gamely wrestling it along the sidewalk. The woman noticed the commotion and spoke: "I very much admire your dog. Poodles have a wonderful sense of humor."

"Your daughter is very much a fan of hers," I returned.

All the color left her face and she stared at me with an expression the like of which I've never seen. The dog took this moment as a sign to sit.

"I mean the girl who lives in your house. Perhaps she's not your daughter."

The woman had been holding one of those Japanese gardening knives. She looked at it in her hand, then at me and the sitting dog. I thought she was going to throw it at me. But what she did was drop it, turn, and practically run back into the house. What had I said?

That afternoon I was busy at my writing desk when I heard the dog scrabbling at the front door. Someone was on the porch. I told the dog to go into her crate and prepared myself to get rid of a solicitor. But it was the gardening woman. She was peering in the door as if she couldn't see – even after I opened it.

"Oh, there you are. May I come in for a moment?"

"Of course. I want to apologize – I must have said something to upset you, Mrs..."

"Hadley. Grace Hadley. And you are ... . . I've looked you up in the neighborhood directory. What I've come to tell you may explain. My daughter Janine is dead. She was killed in an automobile accident three years ago."

We were standing in the middle of the living room. I remember thinking that it was lucky the cleaning lady had made the house presentable just the day before. It wouldn't do to have this conversation in a messy room. I asked Grace Hadley if she would like to sit down.

"No. I felt my behavior was inexcusable. You mistook my house for another, I'm sure."

"Yes, I must have. I'm so sorry."

"She was on her way back to college in Ohio. She was a music student. There was a storm and her car hydroplaned."

"Please, you must sit down."

"No, I'll go now."

At the door I couldn't help myself. "Mrs. Hadley? What instrument did she play?"

She smiled for the first time. "She played the violin. She played very well." Then she turned and walked away, holding the railing as she went down the steps, taking each step carefully.

The dog stirred in her crate so I let her out. She dashed to the door so she could watch the woman walking away through the clear glass, not minding the dog nose smudges. I hadn't mistaken the house.

I had conversations with a girl who might have been Janine. That same girl played the violin. She was familiar and seemed to know me. Or else she was – here I have to say mentally challenged.

I am being challenged mentally by all of this. Mrs. Hadley came to my door to apologize after having serious thoughts of plunking me with a Japanese gardening knife.

Did I have conversations with Janine? Did Mrs. Hadley tell the truth? Do ghosts drive cars?

These were the questions I asked myself after Grace Hadley's visit. I didn't have answers for any of them, and as I scratched the dog's ears, and realizing they were quite ragged, got her brush and worked on smoothing them out – I resolved to walk her in the alley where we saw the cheerful girl. Yes, I allowed to myself and to the dog, I am being a busybody. This isn't any of my business. But my routine involves walking the dog several times a day. It's good for the dog, and it's good for me.

In the alley again. Is it a different squirrel running along the tops of fences behind each lot, or the same squirrel determined to watch a dog pull the arm off a dog walker? Rather dark today, clouds gathered low over us. The birds are quiet, too. A single starling whistles. I raised one when I was a young man living in Philadelphia. It had fallen out of the nest but couldn't fly. Dog food did the job. Her back gate is open – it's the kind of gate that's motorized, rolls slowly open. The old woman who lived in this house before the Hadleys moved in complained to me about how slow it was.

There was no car parked in the open space and the garage door was open and empty. A very clean, uncluttered garage. As curious as I was, I decided to move on. Charlotte was even more curious than I, so I had to give her a tug. Her collar, made of pinched links, simply dropped off. Maybe I hadn't fastened it properly. I looked at the dog, wondering for a moment, an instant, really whether to just gather her up or order a sit. The dog was not only faster on her feet than I – she thought faster. She bolted. But not down the alley, she bolted into the Hadley backyard. She stopped at the back door and did an excited spin. Then, as if she had done it before, she nosed the door and it opened. It must have been partially open because now it stood open about the width of a standard poodle. A poodle no longer in sight because it had disappeared into the house.

This had happened to me once before – we had been on an outing in a snowy field in mid-winter in Ohio where I was teaching at the time. I used to commute weekly – I called myself a migrant fiction worker. The collar fell off and Charlotte began capering around me in the snow, completely aware that I could not catch her. I just turned around in the field and started walking and she followed me obediently.

"Charlotte, come here!" I called to the door of the house, already feeling an equal mix of uncomfortable and foolish. The door, if anything, had swung closed. Stuffing her leash in my pocket, I walked across the threshold of the sliding gate, crossed the backyard and knocked on the Hadley's back door. It was obviously closed. My smart dog could not turn a doorknob. After what seemed like five minutes of knocking (probably one minute), I tried the door. It was unlocked.

I was looking into a mudroom with an open doorway to a large kitchen.

"Hello. My dog has run into your house. Charlotte, come!"

I got no answer. I walked into the kitchen. At this point, I realized, the homeowner had the right to defend property with a weapon. Maybe Charlotte had run out the front door.

The kitchen was not lighted and it was a dark day. I walked past the island toward a hallway and a staircase.

"We're up here!" a cheerful voice came from above me. A female voice. Perhaps the voice of a young girl.

"Is Charlotte up there?" I called from my precarious breaking-and-entering position at the bottom of the stairs.

No reply.

Ignoring an urge to leave the house the way I came in – maybe I could dash home and call the police – I started up the stairs.

Then a bright chandelier of hanging globes making not so much light as glare and primly sitting on a chair, the girl. The room empty save for that wooden chair and another facing it, empty. The chandelier directly above her, glowing but drawing the light out of the room, its window to the outside world almost dark. And on the floor at her feet, my dog, sleeping.

She smiled at me that old smile. I can't see what she is wearing. Something dark, all the light taken out of it. The dog rolled over on her back.

"She likes it here," she said to me.

"You never told me your name."

"I did, but you have forgotten. Sit down. This chair is for you."

I sat in the chair, facing first my sleeping dog, then this girl, and over us, the lights bright and not bright at all.

"Is it Janine?" I asked.

She nodded her head. But it was clear she wanted me to say something more.

"I remember seeing you in the alley, but I should remember you from before."

Again she nodded her head.

"Is this a game?" I asked.

"You knew me a long time ago," she said. "We were in a lovely place at the top of a hill. We made up stories. In the spring there were thousands of dandelions."

"I remember girls. Every old man does. But those girls are women now. Old women. The Irish call them wise women. Do you know what your mother told me?"

Now she was in a different place – and sitting in a rocking chair. She was farther away from us. I say "us" because Charlotte had raised herself in that way dogs have of doing the back and then the front half. She rested her head in my lap.

"She is unhappy," the girl said, and for the first time did not smile at me.

"Is there something I can do to help?"

"You have already. You've brought me to it."

"I don't understand."

Now the dog was staring at the girl as if she was seeing her for the first time. Her tail began to wag.

"Something you don't remember," she said. "Or maybe you never knew."

Then the light above us went out and the room was almost dark. A little gray light came in the window to reveal an empty rocking chair – and opposite the chair I was sitting in, another empty chair. The dog looked around the room – she looked at the ceiling, for all the world as if she were looking in a tree for a squirrel.

"Who's there?" The mother's voice.

* * *

It was the coldest winter in a dozen years my colleagues told me. And it had been cold enough to freeze the pipes in my little rental house while I was away for Christmas break. While the house was being dried out, the college put me and my dog up in a motel. Every day we would walk in the fields between the Inn (as it was called) and a small river that twisted nearby. We trudged through deep snow, Charlotte burrowing with her nose, then shaking her head and snorting. Midway between the Inn and the river, the dog's collar fell off. Probably I hadn't fastened the link properly. At first she dashed in circles around me. I called her and she almost decided to come. But then she charged off toward the river.

In the summer, the river is all fallen trees and roots and deer climb the crumbling earth banks, leaping each time footing fails. Now all that was hidden in snow and ice. When I got to the edge of the steep bank, she was nowhere in sight, but I had been able to follow her tracks. Then I saw her below me, nosing along the ice. Wind had blown the snow off the river. Then she was out on the ice – how thick could it have been – there was a channel of unfrozen water closer to the other bank. I slid down the bank feet first, still calling her. Snow filled my boots. Then I saw she was in the water swimming. I ran out on the ice. The ice broke beneath me and I felt the shock.

It had been so cold that week the ice on my car windows was an inch thick.

When I put the key into the lock of my little hillside rental house, I heard a noise. Briefly I wondered, but when I opened the door, I could see the water pouring from the overhead light fixture. I couldn't turn off the water because the basement door was padlocked, an insurance precaution because the basement stairway had no handrail. I had to drive up to the college at the top of the hill and find security. The officer was on the phone. I wondered if I should interrupt him. I waited.

* * *

Now I think about my students in Ohio. Janine was one of them. She was in one of my writing classes. One day, for no reason, she stood up in the workshop and recited that Yeats poem, "The Stolen Child," from memory.

Come with the fairies hand in hand,

For the world is more full of weeping than you can understand.

That's not right, of course. My memory's faulty. I'm here in this place with the dog. Every day seems the same. Three years ago I was teaching those classes. That winter was so cold. If only the dog hadn't run away.

The Window

The stained glass window was the only thing in the house that James thought he would like to keep after his father died. It was about four feet square and it contained a rather ordinary fleur-de-lis, but it had been the window in his bedroom when he was growing up. Before the sale of the house was final, he arranged to have the window removed and replaced. His lawyer engaged workmen to remove the window, and James made the seven-hour drive to the small town he had once worked so hard to escape.

James spent the night in a motel, and drove to his parents' house early – but an hour after the workmen were supposed to arrive, he was still waiting. James had had the devil's own time of it getting in the front door which had swollen and stuck. It was an oversized door with a heavy glass oval with the etched initials WW, probably belonging to the first owner. James realized that he had never thought about the name in all the years he had lived in the house. Here he was, tugging at the door like a burglar, a burglar in his own house. It was sad inside, the rooms empty and dim – and there were tokens of his father – the large nail he used to lock the screen door from the inside, keys on windowsills. The stained glass window in the back bedroom seemed the same, but the room itself had shrunk. It was hard to picture the furniture in it; it was hard for James to picture himself in it, practicing the flute, studying his Latin: *hic, haec, hoc; huius, huius, huius.*

There was an odd sound which seemed to come from the upstairs. James wondered whether there were vermin in the house. The old circular staircase certainly was noisy enough. He might as well announce himself with trumpets. Upstairs, the rooms were hot and smaller still. The old carpet was thin and didn't protect the floors from squeaking. He thought as he tried to stand silently that he could not remember another carpet – this one had likely never been replaced during his lifetime. There was that sound again, a kind of muffled flurry still coming from above his head. There was a small stairway to the attic floor, dusty and dark, but quieter than the large stairs. James climbed silently until he could see into the attic space – then a sudden rush of wings and insipid cooing – pigeons – he might have known. He had driven them out for his parents five years before – it had been simple, really, a window had swung open. He had only to close it and turn the latch. But this time it was worse. There were piles of guano everywhere and several broken panes in the windows. One had broken in just this moment as an escaping pigeon mistook it for an open space. James' heart was beating as fast as the wings. There were still a few boxes standing next to the brick chimney – old books, mildewed covers, and everything decorated with pigeon shit. James pushed one of the boxes in front of the small window with the broken panes. It might not keep them out but it would present an obstacle. This wasn't going to be his house to worry about. He hated the sound, that syrupy sweet cooing. And the dust, seething and stirred by the pigeons' panic.

There was knocking from downstairs – the workmen had arrived. In the course of the afternoon, the old window was removed, reinforced in temporary framing, and placed into a crate which fit barely in James' van. By evening the new window was in place and the workmen were gone. James prepared to lock up the house one last time.

There was a throbbing, fluttering noise. The pigeons were back in the attic.

"Fine," James said aloud, ignoring the impulse to climb the stairs and roust them out.

"It may be fine for you," a voice said.

James startled, then turned around slowly, scanning the empty room. One of the workmen?

"I've got important papers," the voice said. It was in the room, but not coming from anywhere in particular. This was an old house, empty, save for a few boxes and the dust, which was being fanned into a Kansas windstorm by the pigeons' wings up in the attic.

"Important papers?" James turned and walked out of the room. He opened the front door and walked out on the porch. There were no chairs, but there was a swing in place at the far end. James sat down. It had been his father's voice. It was almost dark. Bullbats were circling and calling over the empty parking lot. He could see the old air conditioner on top of the movie theater in the next block, shape of a silo, its peeling paint invisible. For a moment, honeysuckle in the air. The swing creaked. He used to hear voices when he was a kid. Invisible playmates. Mr. Something. Mr. Somebody. That was it, Mr. Somebody. It's not that unusual. Stirring of old memories. James reentered the house, stood in the silence, his heart not pounding, but swelling, expanding. Then he began to feel settled – no, not settled, tired. He climbed into the attic, pulled the string on the single bulb which did not light, cursed, went down to the kitchen where he knew there was a flashlight. Climbed to the attic again and removed the box blocking the window, the pigeons not panicking this time, merely stepping and fluttering and cursing in their soft soggy syllables. James took the box downstairs, holding his head to the side to avoid the bird dust and placed it in his van. Then he brought down the other two boxes. The house was dark. He drove away without locking it.

The framed window ended up as a hanging piece in James' study. The clockmaker who had restored his father's one handed clock referred him to a stained glass expert who told him the window would have to be rebuilt piece by piece and that it simply wasn't worth the trouble. A storm window had protected it in his parents' house for the last fifty years or it would have collapsed of its own weight. The frame was a nice compromise, but James must understand that the window was old and fragile, that it could still begin to fall apart of its own volition.

The place James chose for it, hanging over the top of the large central window in a bank of three in his studio, allowed it to color the afternoon sun just as it had in his old room in Missouri. James left the dirty boxes of books and papers in the back of his garage, next to a pile of fence posts he was meaning to have hauled away.

Afternoons, James would pull the curtains so that only the stained glass window admitted light into the room. Gradually, the room would take on a peach colored tint, which would deepen to rose, then blood red. James could read, or just sit in the large rocking chair which had once been his mother's favorite. He was hoping to begin work on a book, perhaps a novel. It was there, waiting to be discovered, he was sure of it. He had found stories like this before, waiting them out in silence. He watched the light change each afternoon.

"Remember when we ran out of gas?"

"Which time was that?" James had replied without thinking, as if a conversation had been going on with someone. But there had been a voice, his father's voice, he was certain of it. Now as he sat in the silent house, he examined the echo of his own voice. *Which time was that?* He could play it over in his mind in a quiet place like this. It began to sound to him a great deal like his father's voice. When his father was alive, everyone remarked at how similar their voices were. When he was visiting, he could not answer the phone without being mistaken for his father. Once, answering the phone, in an attempt to head off the mistakes, he lowered his voice, changing his customary greeting – the caller thought it was his mother. James had enjoyed telling the story.

So the voice had been in his head and he had spoken to it. Some story was coming to the surface – soon he would be reading it aloud, changing the sentences, moving paragraphs, revising.

It might well be the story of a time he and his father were driving to St. Louis. His father would drive him twice a month for his music lesson. It might be about his flute teacher whose three cats walked on the tables. There was a coffee table in her apartment surfaced with a home-made mosaic. Little stones in different shapes and colors glued to the surface. It was unfinished, James remembered. For two or three years it had remained unfinished. James could remember what the place smelled like. It smelled like dishes in the sink and cat boxes – not like his home with the deep carpets downstairs not even showing footprints, where there was no dust, no ashes in the ash trays. James always breathed deeply when he came in the door of his teacher's apartment.

But that wasn't the story. He was old enough to drive. He had his license – he had taken driver's ed. But his father said the only real driver's ed would be with him. So he was driving and his father was sitting on the passenger side of the car. Was it the old Desoto? His father yelling at him. Because he's not passing? It's the old two-lane road, US 40. James thinks it's safer not to pass. Or it's nighttime and he has forgotten to switch on the bright beams. There is a button on the floor. He has to jab at it with his foot. How could he describe what his father is doing? Is he yelling or screaming? What does he say? Is there profanity? No, it's not profanity, but the words won't come. James can hear the voice, its pitch, balanced between anger and impatience and desperation. A voice swung wildly like a club. James' shoulders are hunching protectively. The room is red now, but only for a brief moment. Now it's dark and James switches on the light. He hasn't written anything yet – this is preliminary – he'll know when to start.

This day, the next, he wonders about hearing voices. It's nearer noon and there's no color in the room. He's not reminded of his childhood. There's just a big square window hanging with pieces of colored glass that some workman, long dead, assembled, probably after a plan. He probably made dozens of windows just alike.

"Remember the time?" James says this to the empty room, trying out his voice.

"Remember when we ran out of gas?" He can hear a robin outside singing its tattered little song. If he were to draw it, it would be a series of little curlicues. "Remember when you would yell at me, and then pretend you hadn't?" James began to think about inflection, about the way questions end in an up trailing tone. Perhaps the robin is asking questions. Never an answer then. Perhaps then, another tack. "I remember." He says this with a firmer voice. "I remember everything." Even the robin is silent now. More time is passing.

"Spare the rod," a voice, not his, says.

"Spoil..." *Spoil spoil spoil.* He can't understand how it is that he answers that voice so quickly. He can't stop himself. It says (his father's voice, certainly not his father) "spare the rod" with such certainty. Thoughtlessly. The way one might recite a limerick. And James had said "spoil" before he could stop himself. There was no rod, no belt. James could only remember a switch once. The man hit with his hand, in passion. If James had said "Knock knock," he would have hit as soon as "Who's there." Now it had grown dark but the window still had a little glow of pink and green. Poor old window, so many years of watching the light change.

The next morning the lawyer called and reported there was a hitch in the sale of the house. The sump pump had stopped working and half the basement was flooded. The buyer hadn't known about the spring that appeared and disappeared like hives as James' father used to say. Also, he was complaining about pigeons in the attic.

"Tell him he can have the pigeons as a bonus," James said – "and tell him he can set up a water wheel in the basement. He can grind corn. And tell him he can kiss my ass."

The lawyer made some remark about the acorn not falling far from the tree and reminded James that he was paying for the phone call. James thanked him, and leaving the phone off the hook, went for a walk.

The "important papers" seemed to be bound bundles of receipts his mother had kept over the years. James had dragged the boxes from the garage and began to spread their contents on the back yard grass. Two of them contained nothing but books, books he had read as a child. *Thirty Seconds Over Tokyo. The Fall of Constantinople.* The third contained a small photo album, damaged by both mildew and age, which contained photographs of people James didn't know – perhaps they were of friends of his mother's, his father's youth. Some of the photos had faded to a pale yellow, their contents completely erased. There were several sheaves of purchase records of his mother's china and glass collections – not especially valuable in the eyes of his father, James thought. And an envelope containing two photographs – in one a naked Ken and Barbie hind side foremost and all their clothing displayed around them. In the other more doll clothing, furniture. There was a letter addressed to his father from an antique dealer, explaining why she needed additional information to determine the value of the dolls. James wondered what in the world his father was doing with Barbie dolls. The lawyer, trying to describe his dealings with James' father during the last few months before his brain tumor was discovered, used the adjective "Byzantine." Photographs of dolls always seemed creepy to James, but these two looked like murder victims. There was nothing else, just pigeon guano and the thick black dust which had sifted through the shingles and rafters of the old house. How could there have been anything of value if he was trying to sell dolls? The voice had said important papers.

That afternoon in his studio, the peach colored light had begun to bloom again, and despite several false starts, the story in James' mind was determined to stay buried.

"There were no important papers," James said to the window. "Just some damn Barbie dolls. And I don't remember the time we ran out of gas."

"You were fifteen," the voice said.

"Who are you?" James asked.

"What's left," the voice said.

"Dust and birdshit then." James sat for a while expecting to hear the voice again.

The peach colored light deepened toward rose and fluttered as trees outside moved with the wind and turned their branches.

"I'm going to remember something, aren't I?" The light grew richer and then began to fade. Eventually it was dark inside, and James still sat with his back to the window. A small insect had found its way inside and climbed on the side of the desk. When it reached the top it raised the two long sheathes over its wings in a moment of indecision, then closed them and climbed farther.

"Oh." James spoke softly, turning around to the window.

They had run out of gas on the Calwood Road, a two-lane back road which served as a shortcut from the interstate. It hadn't been the only time James' father ran out of gas. It seemed as if he could never decide how far past E the arrow on the gas gauge would go. James didn't understand – maybe the car ran better if the gas tank was nearly empty. It didn't seem to upset his father. They pulled to the side of the road on the south side of Loutre Creek. There wasn't any traffic so they walked along together. Once they had fished the creek together – it had been in July or August. There were dry stretches, but they wore their waders to protect against snakes and chiggers. When there was a stretch of the creek that wasn't dry, James fished with grasshoppers and caught small perch and catfish, even a few bass. He liked walking along the creek bank and discovering something new around the bend. They had fished there only the one time. James' father preferred big fish. The bridge across Loutre Creek was narrow. Technically it was two lanes, but you wouldn't want to meet a truck there. To the left there was a deep pool and James could see some movement below. Some fish were feeding – it was the time for fish to become active, just before dark. They walked along the road and as it began to rise and twist to the right, there was a farmhouse visible on the horizon, and there was a light in the back window – probably the kitchen. To get to the house, they had to walk across an area which wasn't exactly a field, nor was it a yard. It was filled with old junked cars and farm machinery. The house had been easy to see from the road, but you couldn't see it from the field because there was a valley in the middle. The junked cars were like the bumpers in a pin ball game. They made the place into a maze. Finally the house dogs began to bark and an old man came to the back porch door. James' father waved and after an exchange of conversation in which it seemed to James that he was being blamed for the car running out of gas, the old man invited them inside. After the back porch, they walked through a room that served for some kind of storage, then into the kitchen which smelled like bacon. James could see a plate of bacon rinds on the back of the coal stove. His grandmother used to keep bacon rinds like that. The old man and James' father were talking about somebody in town they were both kin to. "Kinfolk" had always meant this kind of delay to James. Adults talking while he waited. This old man was sitting in shadow, glad, apparently, for company. James answered a few questions, how old he was – 15. What he was doing come summer – he didn't know. He thought the question was about his summer job. He hoped he could just practice. There wasn't as much time for practicing during the school year. Soon they were just voices, touching on cousins and crops and weather. James looked out the window at a field away from the road, sloping down to a line of trees, perhaps one hundred yards away. As the voices droned on, the last light drained out of the sky. There were fireflies in the field and they had all begun to rise. As James watched, he could see them on the ends of the grass and weeds, and he could see them hovering just over the top of the weeds. Then as he watched, they began to rise, and there were more and more of them. As the darkness settled, the fireflies rose higher and higher until some of them were as high as the tops of those distant trees. The meadow had become a field of light.

"Look," said James, unable to restrain himself.

"Come out here," the old man said, and the three of them walked out the front door and onto a surrounding porch. James could see the lightning bugs better from this vantage and it seemed to him he had never seen so many. They made the field glow with reflected light. They swirled above his head, still rising. James felt his father's hand on his shoulder.

He did not remember what followed, that they must have taken a gas can to the car and even returned it to the farm, their drive together the rest of the way home, relating their adventure to his mother. Then there were the years that followed, the years in which his life became his own, always moving toward this moment. He was sitting in the quiet of his study, the light having faded once again. He could feel his father's hand resting on his shoulder. Here was his story. The weight of a man's hand. A child and his father.

"Nothing buried in the basement, then." James did not allow an interrogative inflection. It was a flat statement, but he smiled and rocked back, waiting for a story about Barbie Dolls, or for the window to drop its puzzle pieces in one sad splintered heap, or for the voice to clear its throat. Imagine him in a room with the window of his youth, in the near dark, waiting for something he knew would never happen.

The Hockaday House

own Court Street, the central street of the town, running north and south, James drove slowly, looking around him at the familiar sights. Nothing had changed. Even the view toward the hills in the south of town where you could see a mansion at the top, but only in winter when the trees were bare.

Just off Court Street, James parked his car in what seemed now to be a parking lot for the Baptist Church across the narrow street. He could remember when it had not been paved and when there was a small building which might once have been associated with the large white house he was now watching. In those days it had housed a taxi company. Before, it might have had to do with a groundskeeper. There were slave quarters associated with some of the older homes in the town. The large white house had been his childhood home. Then it had become the place he returned to on holidays and where he sat with his parents on the wide porch evenings while the bullbats from the town's nearby buildings wheeled overhead.

His parents were dead a dozen years now and the house sold and apparently made into apartments. It had been apartments when his parents had first moved in – after a few years, they purchased it for the grand sum of $5000 and continued to rent the upstairs to a family who once tried to keep chickens in the basement. Now James could see a confederate flag draped in one of the upstairs windows. The window was partially hidden by a large oak tree, one that grew from a small patch of ground where James' mother once planted tulips and every spring sent him photographs that could have been of the same flowers. Before he turned the corner and pulled into the lot, James had seen the stained glass window that had colored the afternoon light in his room shades of yellow, rose, and pink. Years of afternoons he had set up his music stand and worked through Anderson Etudes, through Handel and Bach Sonatas, through the Mozart concertos his mother loved. Somehow all that music still haunted the big white house, only grown too faint for human ears. There were birds in the oak tree, noisy in the late morning heat. The tenants were all probably at work. James had come to this place, this small town in central Missouri, on his way to Nebraska. There was time along the way to visit this place. What had he planned to do – go inside? No, his destination was a block away, another house like this one, where his best high school friend Larry's mother still lived, now nearing ninety. But first he would rest a moment in the shade of the oak tree with its squabbling birds.

He drove the short block he had often ridden on his bicycle. He drove past the patch of someone's front yard where he had fallen the time his basket support came loose and caught in the spokes of his front wheel. He had taken a foot-long divot that day. And in the story he told after, the wheel had lost all its spokes. Now the corner house, somewhat overgrown, and its paint, white with brown shutters, could stand refreshing. James thought the old lady lived alone. Larry, who still played in the orchestra James had quit the year his father died, often spoke of her – but James hadn't mentioned to him this planned visit. He still wasn't sure. Maybe he would sit here in the car and watch the house behind the high and unkempt boxwood hedge. Larry's mother was called Kay. Even Larry called her Kay. Kay had played the organ in the Methodist Church until she retired years ago. Her husband Jerry had given James his first flute lessons. Mr. McDonald. Dead these twenty years. A stern unsmiling fellow who failed to notice that James hadn't learned to read music – that he was playing by ear. And now Larry looked exactly like him. Sometimes that resemblance startled James. The house was quiet – no birds in the heat-wilted trees, no traffic on the street. Mr. McDonald had had an enormous LP collection of jazz from the 40's and 50's. James and Larry had listened to them all. More music to haunt old rooms. With that thought to comfort him, James climbed out of the car and walked to the opening in the hedge where a narrow sidewalk climbed up to the front porch. The hedge needed trimming and scraped his right arm. Whisper of boxwood leaves.

James crossed the porch and rang the bell. There were some old garden tools arranged in a corner. *Dorbel,* an odd word, meaning a dull-witted pedant, foolish pretender to learning. Words. James kept old dictionaries and collected the words. The door opened. An old woman with a cane emerging from the dark. *Ruse the fair day at night.* Ruse means praise.

"May I help you?" Her eyes were the same eyes James remembered: clear, intelligent. She had taught in the college, perhaps music history.

"Mrs. McDonald. I was passing through town. I wonder if you remember me, Larry's friend?"

She frowned at him, perhaps because of the light behind him. *The fair day.* "Oh it's James, then. James, the flute player. You've come to see the old woman."

Ruse, roos, royse, rowze, reouse, reeze. James watched her in her dark doorway telling his word beads, unsettled. I've come to see the old woman, he thought, but did not say. He did not say anything, which was increasingly strange. His fingers made patterns of flute notes in the palms of his hands.

"Are you going to come in? Or have you finished with me?"

"I wanted to see you again," James said, returned to the moment. "Yes, yes, if you have the time."

"I have little else," the old woman said, and she led him into the dark house, dressed in her dark old-woman's clothes, leaning on her cane. Her hair was braided and arranged like a round hat on her head, abundant. And her face was oddly smooth. While she leaned on the cane, she seemed to move swiftly – through a dining room with a walnut table, then through a small kitchen, which was neat and clean. She seemed to be taking him on a tour of the house. Finally she stopped in a den or library, a place with many books, but also many photographs. Stuffed chairs and rocking chairs. The stuffed chairs were decorated with lace throws. There were figurines on some of the shelves. Collected like words. But in more danger. The books on the shelves above the figurines had bowed the shelves down. Someday the shelf would collapse and crush them – what were they? Children, a goose girl. Dogs and pigs. A musician, a cocky fellow, playing a violin. The kinds of figures his mother had kept.

"Do you remember Mary Liz? Weren't you in the children's choir? She passed away last month. My last old friend." They were sitting down, James in a rocking chair. And the small talk simmering. James' share was nodding. The old woman sat bolt upright and spoke concisely, her voice pitched like a singer's, or like someone who was slightly deaf.

"And Larry hung a bird feeder for me. The old enjoy watching birds he's been told. Do you see the birds?"

Outside a pleasantly lace-curtained window, breaking the monotony of the shelves and admitting very little light, James could see a hanging bird feeder, of the kind that protect against squirrels. There were no birds, and the feeder seemed to contain no seeds.

"I think you have run out of seeds. I could fill it for you."

"And then the birds will come and the old lady will watch the birds at their breakfasts." Her eyes were dark – she had always been a busy woman, allowing the boys the run of the house. *Housel*: To administer. The house houses, James thought. Not merely contains. It marshals the dust motes and the mice.

Kay had gone to the kitchen because of the teakettle. A cat scuttled away. No mice then, James thought. What had she said about the birdseed when he offered to fill the feeder a second time? A harrumph. A teacher's dismissal.

Tea. No sugar, thank you. A cardinal lit on the feeder momentarily. A female in dull clothing. James thought he might point it out, but it flitted away. *Dul...dulcarnon*. At wit's end.

"Did you see your house – your old house? Those people living there cook meth." Kay slurped her tea and set down the cup, pushing the saucer so near the edge of the little cherry side table they were sharing, James had to grab for it to avert disaster.

"Meth?" he repeated stupidly.

Another sharp look. "Are you paying attention, young man?"

"I'm sorry. I didn't expect you to know about such things. And I'm sorry the house is made up into apartments."

"They will tear it down if they don't blow it up before," Kay said, continuing to relish her tea. Her teeth were a bit too regular and large for her face. Teeth don't shrink.

"...one house in this town that is worth preserving."

Again he had missed something. The bending bookshelf bowed itself over the figurines. A trick of light.

"Jefferson Davis slept there in 1875. There's one thing I want to see before I die. And it's not birds' breakfasts."

"Why not, then?" James said. A house she wants to see. "In this town, there's a house you haven't seen inside?"

"Fifty years ago I had the chance... but I didn't take it." She lunged for her cane, upsetting the tea things this time for certain. James was immediately ashamed of the way he had dodged backwards instead of reaching to save the day again.

"Leave it. Leave it. You are absolutely right. We won't be able to get in, but we can see the garden. On the other hand... Jerry had a key..." She sailed into the last of the downstairs rooms, one in which a baby grand piano stood like a mother duck guarding piles of books which had been crowded under it. In one corner there was a peg board decorated with a plethora of keys.

Following her, James thought the keys looked like fishing lures – they seemed tangled and hopeless. He left her jangling and rattling them. Only one cup was broken. He scooped up the mess and took the intact cup and saucers to the kitchen. The tea was cold. *Keel.* To cool by stirring. And the keys keel. An old lady's wind chimes. Then in the doorway. An old lady triumphant. Kay's keys.

"Now, she said, almost grandly. Take me to the Hockaday house." James realized finally the house she meant. In wintertime, you could see it if you looked south at the hill that rose beyond Town Creek. A silhouette on the hill's very top – a very large house it had seemed to James the boy. But he had never explored that part of town. Not even when he had a paper route? He had. There was a gate and a huge lawn. But the house was hidden by trees from that direction, too. You couldn't get near it. And now, as they drove through the two blocks of the business district, you couldn't see it behind the almost black tint of the summer trees.

Behind them, in the library with the tea spilled on the floor, the shelf above the figurines omitted a loud crack, startling a cat. But no books fell.

Even with the seatbelt fastened, Kay seemed to sit bolt upright in the passenger seat. There was no conversation as they passed the bank where James' mother had been a secretary, then an officer, then down to the bridge over Town Creek and up the hill. This was a hill so steep, James had never been able to ride his bicycle up it; and, in fact, it had seemed too steep to ride the bike down.

James turned left at Kay's direction. Larry had mentioned her driving only a few years before. Then they reached a gateway with a small gatehouse and a low stone wall marking the property. The wall had not been well maintained and was rather weedy and strewn with saplings. The gate was open and there was a relatively intact blacktop driveway which disappeared into a grove of large oaks and maples.

"Do drive on. There's nothing to be seen from here." James could see a rectangle of lighter color which indicated that some kind of plaque had once been in place on the brick gate post.

"Is this one of those places on the National Registry?" James asked.

"No, not any more. Be careful now. Just beyond these trees."

And beyond the trees James let his car roll to a halt. He was looking at half a house. Perhaps two thirds. It was offering its profile and the back of the house was a ruin.

"No, no. Keep following the drive." Kay actually swatted him on his arm in her enthusiasm.

James drove on and the driveway was studded with patches of grass and weeds but it continued around to the back of the house. From this perspective, the condition of the house was not so drastic – a two story porch had either collapsed or someone had begun to demolish it and given up. Only the roof remained and although it was buttressed by timbers, it had pulled partly away from the house. A few more good rains, James thought.

"That porch roof looks dangerous, but from the driveway it looked like the whole house was falling down," James said.

Kay unfastened her seat belt. "It was sold to a speculator and now it is a scandal. The city would like to buy it, but everything is tied up in court. Come with me – I may have a key that works." Kay lifted a huge purse, a bag constructed of some kind of quilted material, and James could hear the jangling of many keys.

James had to take her arm and assist her through what once might have been a classical arrangement of decorative boxwoods. The plants were healthy enough but they had grown leggy and the obvious pathway was often obscured by the growth.

"Nature's own topiary," Kay remarked as they backtracked to skirt one particularly enthusiastic obstacle. "There's an entranceway past this damaged area – see the steps. And everything is stone here. This is where I want to try Jerry's keys"

"Why would you have keys to this house?" James was beginning to feel like an accomplice in a criminal trespass. "And why doesn't the city just condemn the place?"

"My late husband... when he was a young man...had an arrangement with the mistress of the house. He was a kind of caretaker. All that came to an ending as all things will. And there are more stories than there are true stories. Here. Please hold my bag." She steadied herself with her cane.

And the old lady insisted that James hold the bag as if he were holding yarn for her knitting. And from it she fished keys – keys that had been strung on chains as if they were Christmas tree ornaments – and one by one she tried them in the door lock – adroitly, skillfully, it seemed to James. Little metal scraping sounds counterpointed her intense breathing. She had a smell, James realized – a rather sharp order, one he would not have associated with human origins, something like a mink, James imagined, or perhaps a fox, something fierce.

"There!"

The door swung open. They were in an alcove, partially hidden from view, a fact which had eased James' mind to some extent of the consequences of his role as bagman. The door, although some kind of service entrance, was oversize and rounded at the top, reinforced with metal straps that would have served a dungeon handsomely. A robin twittered from the direction of the boxwoods, taking the place of any sound the hinges might have omitted.

"Now the old woman will see the Hockaday house." Kay delivered the line in a whispered soliloquy – and then, in a perfectly normal, if only slightly theatrical voice, addressed James: "Young man, please bring my bag along. There may be other locks."

They entered a kitchen. There were small high windows which supplied some light. As large as the house seemed – as large as it must have been, this was a small kitchen. There were many cabinets and two sets of sinks, but no appliances.

"The front of the house will be more interesting. Come along." And the old lady moved off briskly.

James stopped at a dumb waiter. There was apparently a lower level as well as an upper dining level. The shaft was empty. In the dim light of the kitchen, and the quiet of the house, James felt peaceful, almost drowsy. He had been driving for hours. Now he was escorting a crazy old lady through... he looked at the shadows thrown on a wall of cabinets by a window guarded by some kind of grillwork... through a gingerbread house. *Gin*: cunning. *Quaint of gin*. A trap that springs.

There was a sharp noise from the front of the house. Slamming door? Something fallen? James hurried through the hallway Kay had taken. Another room, larger than the kitchen, the purpose of which wasn't apparent. Nobody there.

"Kay, where are you?" James called.

James listened for some reply. He could hear only something faint. A dragging sound. Then silence. He had come to a narrow stairway. Up or down? Up. The stairway turned and was almost completely dark – James felt his way holding the banister. Then light again from the top of the stairway. Much more light. And birds. Sparrows from the sound of it, chirping in a large space, a little echoey.

James found himself in a great room with a huge fireplace at the far end. Large windows admitted bright afternoon light. It was, in fact, hot in the room – the kitchen had been cool. There were a few large pieces of covered furniture and there was a long table, like a library table, in the center of the room. And arranged around the bare fireplace, a row of chairs. Sitting in one, an old lady in black – and in another, a girl of perhaps twelve years, with very thin bare arms and a green dress. She had long blond hair and she was engaged in what seemed to be a whispered conversation with the old lady.

"James, my bag. Bring me my bag," the old lady called to him from across the room which James could now see was populated in its upper parts by sparrows, calling loudly and flitting about. A window must be broken.

Who is that child? What bag?

"James, my bag." An imperious old woman, waving her cane.

The bag by the dumbwaiter in the kitchen. Perfectly natural to find Kay with a girl in a green dress in a room full of sparrows. James wondered as he felt his way down the darkened elbow of stairs if there was a way to free the sparrows. But perhaps they were at home in the house. They had seemed so cheerful. Cheerful. That's the word. Little points of bright sound. Nattlesome, of course. Quarrelsome. And outside, the robins prowling among the sprung boxwoods. Scribbles of robin song. A scribble is a mild scrabble.

Scratch and claw. And the bookcase in Kay's house. Odd thought. There, the bag. Heavier than it had been – as if it held books. Keys and books. Books are keys. In Kay's house, the bookcase tumbling out its books. The confederate flag like a sail, blowing out that upstairs window and glass following, hung then in the oak tree, and black smoke. A sound you couldn't hear all this way apart, at the top of the great hill over town creek. But one which rattled Kay's bookcase – and the books spilling down, making this bag feel so heavy, here climbing the dark stairs again.

In the sparrow room, then. The sparrows silent and the light different. The walls are a cream color. Had he noticed that? The bag so large and, of necessity, dragging behind him.

Where is Kay? Where is the little green girl? The huge fireplace, arched at the top, but so high a man could walk inside. And the chairs. Set against the wall as if at a dance. Sarabande, minuet, slip jigs and reels, polka, pooka...

A dull thud, muffled by distance. Blasting perhaps. Construction? In the old days there were mines about: clay, gypsum. How did they dig them? Old lady and green girl. Dragging bag. Upstairs then. Sisyphus.

James walked to the front of the house, dutifully carrying Kay's bag of keys. There was a wide and curving staircase but the light was muted. Sparrows began to tune again from the great room. Whatever had passed had passed. The air was light now. Across from the Methodist church, flames flickered from the large white house. The stained glass window, old when that room belonged to James, had crumbled behind its storm window outer shield. Fire engines. Burly young men with short haircuts. To prevent elflocks. Knots twisted by elves. A burler pours out ale. Burl ale on the knots, then.

These stairs are dusty but not dark. A few scattered leaves. Oak and elm perhaps. Now, sitting rooms, some light, some not. A library with a second story, a gallery. But where are the books – all the fairy tales? Quiet room, tables and chairs uncovered, its far corners dark, too dark.

"Hello. Is there someone there?"

Something unmoving. Stuffed bear with that arched open mouth and ritual display of teeth. It's the neck that is arched but the mouth strains, too. Some kind of game. No, nothing there. No bear. Not in this story.

Another sitting room. This one larger with a fireplace almost as large as the one below.

"James, bring me my bag."

James looks around the room where there is enough light to see there is no one dressed even in black nor girl in green but there is in a far corner in a pale pool of light a small piano – no, make that a harpsichord. No cover and no dust. Where is that old woman? The keyboard cover is locked down. No, just stuck. James tries a note. Ahh. Dead and flat. Like a bad smell. Too bad. But it could be restrung.

James walks the length of the floor, peering into rooms and then up the narrow stairs to the top story, feeling his way. Here are little cells, servant's rooms. Monk dens. But no monks, no bears either. Shelter. Hovels are shelters. To hove is to take shelter. Den up. Where have the servants gone? Then he hears the music, the harpsichord, only a little flat, floating up from the sitting room. It's the Aria of the Goldberg Variations.

At this distance, the harpsichord sounds almost grand, even if it's old pitch flat.

One more room. Here's where the porch attached. Hanging canvas. The floor might give way. Back to the stairway.

At the harpsichord then, the old woman.

"That's lovely. Did you know there was an instrument here?"

"When I was a girl, I would often dream," Kay said, "of an old empty house which was filled with ghosts. But the ghosts were made of music. At night the music came out... in the day, too, I suppose. But there was no one to play it. We don't make the music you know..." Kay took her bag from James and then closed the keyboard and applied a small key to the lock. Taking his arm, she walked with him toward the large staircase, leaning slightly against him, as if she were weary. Her cane is nowhere to be seen.

"There was a girl in a green dress."

"A girl?"

"Sitting with you and whispering."

"If there had been a girl, I would have said she told me she plays here sometimes, that there is an unlocked window in the back, or a French door..."

"I saw a girl in a green dress."

"You saw a ghost, then."

"Why do you have keys to this house?"

They were walking together down the stairs. An old woman in black. James carrying her bag of keys.

"I want you to speak to Larry," Kay said. "He does not visit me. It's not good to leave an old woman alone.

"I wish you would tell me what you know about this house," James said as they retraced their path through the kitchen. Several of the cabinet doors stood open and James closed them, suspecting that, afterward, they would spring open again.

"Larry's brothers are no better," Kay complained, her voice becoming more querulous. "I know I complain. What else is there for me to do?"

"Will you tell me the story of the girl in the green dress?"

James opened the large arched door and held it for his companion.

"Give me the key and I'll tell you the story."

James looked into the bag he was carrying. It must have contained 40 keys.

"Young man, let's make a beginning of it. We can't leave the house unlocked. Someone will steal the harpsichord."

James handed her a key. After trying it in the lock, she dropped it on the brick path.

"Well, give me another. The girl's name is Abigail. She lives in a story with a hedgehog and a teakettle. Give me another."

James could smell a mimosa tree. He looked about him but could not see one. Key clink, continuing. He handed them mechanically. Keys are mechanical.

"Let me see. No bears. I'm certain of that. Another key, if you please. There. There! Now we can go to market. Leave those keys. They will not open anything."

And during the short ride down the hill and across Town Creek and up Nichols Street to 8th, James heard more about a turnip which would not come out of the ground no matter how many of Abigail's friends assisted each other in pulling it.

Excerebrate: To clear out the mind. And then what floods in? Old stories?

Up the steps then with the old lady, past the overgrown boxwood hedge, infested, James noticed, with vines.

"Will you have a cup of tea?"

"No thank you, Mrs. McDonald."

"You are a formal young man, aren't you? Thank you for the picnic."

Kay entered her house, closing the door behind her silently.

Picnic. Pickpocket. Pickpenny. Picklock.

It was not late. James sat in his car. This would be the time to light up a cigarette, but he had never smoked. One more time then. Up to 10th on Nichols, then slowly down Court Street, one way south, passing some of the nicest houses in town. James had admired them every day he walked to school. Then through the business district. At the creek, a block west to the highway, and then across the bridge and up the hill. Where had they turned? Yes. Had he noticed the street sign? *Hockaday Lane.* Hadn't there been a stone wall? What a handsome old house. Well kept yard. Children's riding toys. And there, a girl in a green dress. James stopped his car and got out.

"Hello there," he called in his most friendly voice, keenly aware that he was the stranger children are always taught not to speak to. "Can you tell me where I can find the Hockaday House?"

"I'll ask my mother," she answered brightly and skipped around the side of the house. It was a rather large house and there was a plaque on the side of it which James could begin to read as he moved closer.

At Kay's house again, ringing the bell and knocking on the door behind the boxwood hedge and getting no response. Then the neighbor explaining that the old lady had passed away several months ago. Had James known her?

Yes, but that had been a long time ago. Too long.

Forfare: To pass away, decay, perish.

Driving west across the flat Missouri fields toward Columbia and Kansas City, farmhouses and clumps of trees intensely distant.

Forwander: to weary oneself with wandering.

So many times James had looked up from a moment in his life and seen the white house on the hill, and wondered briefly if he would ever know its stories, its secrets. Then the moment would receive him again.

The Turret House

A place. Let's start with sound. There are lawnmowers spaced like mockingbirds, about one and a half to a block. The mowers come and go – that is, the sound grows louder because someone is walking, that mower-pacing, mind deeply relaxed, eyes following a line of cut grass, the sound I hear muted behind the walls of this house alive out there in the vibrating handle of the machine. The smell of mown grass is rising – currents flow invisibly, intricately. I can take a moment away from these sentences to walk in that world and then return, refreshed.

I have been in this place before and now I return to it. Ohio, Oklahoma, Indiana, Tennessee, Ohio again, cowering in the middle of the alphabet. A village built on a handful of hills in the midst of corn and bean fields. And a house, this one, with its two stories and attic, its wide front porch, slate steps and cracked cement sidewalks. Inside the house, rising above the wide floor planking, the stairs creak constantly. It isn't even necessary to tread on them.

The village is small enough to walk to the post office, to the IGA, the hardware store, but no one walks, of course. Most of the houses are tricked up with Victorian frills, towers, stained glass windows, historical plaques and three-color paint jobs. There are wrought iron fences and picket fences and the smell of fresh paint. Interesting that wrought iron can be painted white but black picket fences are rare.

Now the near mowers are silent, and I can hear the distant mowers. Like sheep on a mountainside, their bleating, their bells. I must begin the story: A child and his father fishing together. Let's say a long time ago. Fifty years is a round number. They wear hip boots and follow a small creek. The bed of the creek is sometimes dry, sometimes yields to pools, sunken bends, meanders. In the deeper pools bluegill, small-mouth bass, catfish, turtles, crayfish, bullfrogs, giant water bugs, hellgramites, and over those same pools dragon flies, damsel flies, mosquitoes, gnats, red-winged blackbirds, the overhanging branches of trees the boy can't identify, but there are willows, birch, and cottonwood.

The boy's eyes are on the water's surface, looking for the slight bulge that might identify a turtle when the snake's striking startles him. A blow against his booted leg and the violence of that writhing escape. Startled, his heart beating like a bell, he still wonders at its thickness, the heft of its strong body amid that snake energy, that exhibitionistic undulation in which it seems to be going several directions at once, the furious slashing toward the water and then swimming, over water, underwater, water moccasin. Snake, snake,

snake he chants to calm himself as he feels the rubber boot for snake fang punctures. He has fallen on the dry creek bed stones, but his leg has no feeling – his body has no feeling. Everything is quiet save the distant chirr of a red-winged blackbird. Where is his father? Dead these ten years. And the snake? There is always a snake.

* * *

The sky is dark today. Everyone's mowing to race the weather. The giant elm in the back yard is palming its leaves toward the cut grass below, anticipating rain. A real train whistle identifies the distance. Boundaries. Most distant, clouds moving this way from the west, less distant, that train, a half dozen blocks. Least distant, the past. Yesterday. Anything on the other side of sleep. Elsa in Tennessee, our son Nate with her. I made my living playing music once. Once I was that fishing boy. Now father to another. There is always a fishing boy. Always a father. Another story: Nate is sitting on the front porch, playing his guitar. He's wearing what he calls hobo gloves; the fingers are cut off at the second knuckle. (That tree behind this house is more than two hundred years old. He has climbed it, found the carved inscription "Derwin." A joke. Welsh for oak tree.) The house, too, has a Welsh inscription. But there's not enough of it to decipher, painted over so many times. Nate then, playing, his left hand flying up and down the neck as if it were free of his wrist. I can't hear the music from here. His story? It's about the old lady across the street – the one who lives in the turret house that's got "Rhaeder" painted over the top row of windows. I've sketched it, and I've got it here somewhere, in a box behind the rocking chair, but one has only to count the windows from this place (this desk, from which I can see the elm he climbed) imagining a labyrinth, moving always to the right – at the seventh window it appears, a white house close to the road, built into the hillside and the old woman, Mrs. Price, Nate will learn, has brought her trash down to the sidewalk because tomorrow is the day the trucks come to pick it up, the Big O trucks. She has closed the lid of her blue dumpster and she's looking across the street at the porch where Nate is playing (I can hear it now) Villa Lobos. She's coming across the street. There's not much traffic this time of day. Just after a rain, a washed and sparkling light dimming and fanning out again as clouds ride above the wind, stretching and yawning.

"Good day, young man."

Nate has stopped playing. For some reason I can't hear what he's saying.

"No, it's not your father that I wish to see. I've seen you playing here these past few weeks, and visiting with your friends. My name is Mrs. Price, and I live across the way. Perhaps you could help me with some boxes I need to move."

Nate is thinking about his friend Carrie who had agreed to come over, and who has taken longer than she promised, this while he says something about the music he's practicing – he's not paying much attention to what he's saying because he's begun to notice this old woman whose name is Clara Price, a widow of twenty-three years, her husband killed at a railroad crossing when his car stalled and he could not resist trying one last time to restart it. The old woman has something between her eyes – what do they call it? A wen. A flappy kind of thing like a remora clinging to a shark. Nate likes the nature shows on TV. Afternoons he watched them with me after his mother first left us.

"Of course, I'll pay you. I just realized today…"

The remora clinging to Mrs. Price gives her a kind of jaunty look. Her white hair seems disorganized in a kind of hedgehoggy way. She's wearing a long black skirt and a dark sweater above it with a white silk scarf around her neck knotted handsomely. Leather shoes with laces peeking out. Nate thinks she's some kind of cross between a pirate and a nun. He can't wait to tell Carrie. And he can't help staring at that flappy thing. There are others, but in less interesting places. Perhaps they move about at night. He looks down the block toward Carrie's house. Nobody.

At the seventh window, see him now, following Mrs. Price across the street, after they both pause for the passing of a large green John Deere combine, a very noisy thing. It's certain they're not talking as it grinds unpleasantly by, both lost in their thoughts.

Five dollar bills in the blue teapot.

Calico cat on the stairway, slinking up. I've seen the cat before, mouse in her mouth. Waiting for the old woman. There must be a sound when they bite through the bones.

Now from the eighth window – I have washed them all, admiring the old glass, its waves and bubbles, like the surface of a spring – see them climbing the stairs to Rhaeder house, flagstone steps. The ninth window is memory. Nate remembers this, will remember me. I'll tell the story first and he'll tell it again.

Nate has thrust his gloves in his pocket, wonders if he should have put the guitar inside the front door instead of laying it on the porch swing. It's a cheap guitar belonging to his father. There's always a father.

"You mustn't mind the house, young man."

She's got loose keys in a pocket. Locks her door to take out the trash.

Where's the cat?

Here's the last thing you can see from the eighth window, Clara Price poking that key the way you'd stoke a coal fire, rattling the door – or was that the combine, now turning at the light, two blocks away?

There's no color, little light, blinds drawn, dust like flour or blown sand. Mouse smell.

"They're in the tower room. I want to bring them down here to the kitchen. Scat, Millicent." Millicent is the cat, her calico bled out, colorless.

The stairway, as Nate had imagined, is steep and turns to the right, making a clock's moves, Nate thinks, then decides he's wrong – it depends on whether you're going up or down. The treads creak like the stairs at home. Another closed door and pocket of keys rattling, bare bulb lit.

"Would you like me to help you with that key?" Nate wonders if she's got the right one. She seems to have a palsy and she's been mumbling little bird-like imprecations, roosting noises, unconscious effort.

Prying the lid off a coffin. Odd thought.

* * *

"A snake bit me," he said, the boy I was.

His father, from the other side of the creek, standing on an elevated clay bank, the sun behind him, and of consequence made to have shining outline but darkness in place of body and face, asked him if he was sure, so many things in the world susceptible to confusion with snakes.

"A snake. A snake. Black. No, brown with patterns. See him swimming. From up there you should be able to see him swimming."

"What kind of patterns? Are you sure you saw a snake?"

"He bit my leg." The boy sits down, suddenly dazed.

His father must, he knows, backtrack through shrubs and rosebushes down to the riffle where he can cross on the white stones.

* * *

A final rattle and the door jerks open, the knob fallen off and bouncing down the stairs past Nate, sounding, in the hollow stairwell with its one worn wobbling banister, like a host of doorknobs, a Biblical doorknob plague. All the doors in this house must be springing open, Nate thinks.

At first old Mrs. Price blocks the doorway.

"Oh damn." In a fluty voice.

Nate is grinning. He can do this voice and Carrie's going to hear this story.

Now there's light; Mrs. Price has flounced, how else to say, through the door. A wall of windows – no shades here. This is the tower top, Nate thinks, noticing at a glance the ceiling, oddly domed and braced, something for the old house shows on TV, but first – windows all around four walls, a square room not especially small, and turned against two, no, three walls – pianos. Keyboards like bad teeth. Uprights and those round piano stools – spin it until it falls off like a doorknob. Some are smaller with organ foot pumps – harmonium. Harmonia? Against the fourth wall, nearly to the windows' tops, the boxes stacked like books – they may be filled with books. Under all that dust, it's hard to tell. Nate can see down to the street, and across, his own house. Small now, like a monopoly house, only the elm behind still huge. He's in a tower on a mountainside.

"What are the pianos for?" Nate asks.

Mrs. Price has settled on a bench and has removed a shoe which seems to have a broken heel. Nate's not looking too closely.

"Oh, Mr. Price collected them."

Too many windows for a boy whose mind is set on wandering – the steep hillside rising behind the stacked-box windows – you can see the switchbacks of a lonely trail of winding steps.

"...and on this one, he wrote 'The Dance of the Blessed Happy Wanderers.' That was just a week before his tragic death."

You can see the whole two blocks of Pearl Street and the Inn at the corner of Broadway with its row of fountains.

Now she's playing something on a piano in a key somewhere between A and B flat. (Nate has perfect pitch.). Nate feels in his pockets for the gloves. He's got one but the other has fallen out, probably on the stairs.

He'll need both his gloves if he's going to move any of those boxes – and that landmine roller-skate door knob, too. *Dark stairwell. The old lady's going for six stanzas for sure.*

* * *

He's not happy, the father, slightly winded from clambering down the steep clay bank, and stepping in a muskrat hole. There is the boy, mooning on a rock, head in his hands.

"Well let's have a look. Take off that boot."

It's not a snakebite, but who could tell? I've managed to scrape my leg on a sharp rock, either when I saw the snake, or just now when I felt dizzy. There's a gash from my ankle to my knee.

"You've done it this time, Thomas. How long did it take? Have we been here a half hour?"

Father and son confer. Son does not feel like walking at the moment, would rather sit. (Would rather be left alone so as not to be seen crying.) Father observes that the gash is not bleeding, but should be washed and bandaged. There's a bottle of hydrogen peroxide in the trunk of the car. Hydrochloric acid. Thomas rocks holding his aching leg. He's sitting on a rock. A rock chair. And the father (just for a moment, until the kid pulls himself together) is fishing at the far end of the pool where something heaved, shouldered its way to have a closer look at his floating lure, then paused, unconvinced. They both wait now: the father, the something. Waiting, the father thinks about his own father, a man of few words, and those less eloquent than the back of his hand. Dead, he won't go away, always lurks in dreams, powerful again – and that father had a father, too. A man with a fine singing voice and a violin. And him the son of … that fish is backing off, but don't twitch the lure yet. Patience. Every one of us a mooning boy.

* * *

"Nathanial." (fluty tones) "Where have you gone?"

"I'm looking for my glove. I dropped it on the stairs."

"Do bring the doorknob if you see it." Sound of sliding cardboard box.

Nate has found a door ajar at the first landing. "Maybe it rolled in here," he doesn't think – he says, preparing his defense.

Table lamps like a school of fish. With those shades like inverted bowls made of colored glass. And little walnut tables. Fringed cloths. Hutches. Armoires. Knickknacks. Porcelain figurines. Glass objects. Objects. At least a dozen lamps (and lit) by the count. And on the tasseled rug, by a seaweed skirl of cat fur, one doorknob. A central aisle which Nate can't help following, magic doorknob in hand. Many shelves but no books. Nate's father has too many books. They're like music his father says. You want to read them again. A small round table with a candle in front of the window. And Nate's glove. The one he must have dropped on the stairs. A candle lit within the past ten minutes or so. And what else? Reading glasses? A drinking glass containing a set of false teeth. Rather important looking on the white doily. This is a long room, Nate thinks, as he takes his glove and begins to walk backwards. Even with all the lamps, or perhaps because of them, it seems especially dark with girder works of shadow. Plenty of places to hide holding a hatchet or perhaps a machete. And past the table with his glove, there was an archway to the right, introducing an area which seemed to Nate completely dark. Room probably for a lurking string quartet of zombies at the very least. Nate has made his way back to the door where he can hear the sound of sliding boxes from above. Perhaps he should have pinched the false teeth.

"I found the door knob."

"Good. Good. Put it in the piano, then."

"In the piano?"

"Yes, dear. With the others."

Still pushing the boxes, she gestures toward one of the uprights. It has no lid. Nate sees inside, to within six inches of the top, door knobs. An ossuary of door knobs. Some glass, some painted, some brass. They are most of them complete, the inside and the outside knob – joined by the knob axel, the door femur, the whatsits. The inside knob is still in the tower room door, Nate notices – wonders if he should bring it to the attention of Mrs. Price.

"Here is the box I've been looking for."

*   *   *

The two make their way along the creek bed, retracing their original path, finding, in fact, a fishing lure which must have dropped out of the son's tackle box. Thomas refuses his father's assistance, feels now this persistent gnawing sensation in his hurt leg, resists the urge to moan, realizes he's doing it anyway.

"It can't be that bad. It's just a scrape."

"Sorry."

The father is a meat cutter, a butcher – but never uses that word. Comes home often with stitches, gashes, portions of fingers sliced, and stories of worse. This is all a cheerful business, this carnage, more interesting than the work of other fathers.

"Why do you keep saying 'sorry'?"

"I don't know. I'm sorry."

They have come to the road, or rather, to the bridge, which has a very steep slope up to the road. There's a dark and broad pool which extends under the old one-lane bridge and for some ways on the other side.

"Look." Thomas has forgotten his leg. A mallard hen and a kite tail of six tiny ducklings swims serenely away from them under the bridge. For Thomas it's a miraculous vision. His father has already climbed to the level of the road and is coaching him to grab the end of a stick he has thrust down toward him. Halfway up the bank, Thomas lets go, slides back down and into the water where he sits, defeated. The ducks have disappeared. The father is quietly swearing.

* * *

This box is larger than the rest although not by much.

"What's in it?" Nate asks. There is someone else in the house, he has decided. Someone in that room downstairs. Just around that corner, in an armchair, in the dark.

"Mr. Price's hobby was carving decoys."

The box is sealed with paper tape which comes off as Nate takes over the task of sliding the box away from its fellows.

Inside the box are some old books, and, notably, a single carved and painted duck. It seems realistic to Nate. And there are baby ducks, ducklings palm-of-the-hand size. And each painted like the large one. All of them have black glass eyes. The big one is mottled, mostly gray with black. The little ones have black horizontal lines extending from their eyes. Some have black patches on the tops of their heads. One is almost completely black. And from each of the ducklings hang treble hooks. They are tricked up like fishing lures. There might be a dozen of them.

"Please, young man, don't touch."

Nate returns the duckling he was holding to the box. The hooks were sharp.

"Where do you want this moved – the kitchen?"

She nods affirmatively.

The box is awkward to hold but it isn't especially heavy. Nate sets it down in the doorway.

"Is there someone else in the house?" he asks her. "Someone in the room with all those lamps?"

"What do you mean – all those lamps?"

* * *

It's another day. It's the same day. The lawn mowers circling and pacing. The trees are a deeper green and the light is hot, falling only upon the just. The birds are in noon-stupor. I'm in the house across the street from Nate and his story, the house where Nate and Thomas lived one time in their lives, the house where I imagined them. Like all things, this house is imaginary. Moving to the right, as is proper with all labyrinths, to the eighth window, you'll see the white turret house. Rhaeder means waterfall. It isn't taking any time for me to tell you this. It's still the same day in the story. And the same time of day. The story is still in Ohio. And in a state of mind. In the limbic system and temporal lobe circling like a child's electric train.

* * *

"The lamps with glass shades," Nate says, "...in the room downstairs, where I found the doorknob."

"Young man, there's no room with lamps. There were lamps in Mr. Price's study, of course, but that room's been closed off since he passed away. Now, if you'll take this box down to the kitchen, I'll give you $5 for your trouble."

Right. No room with lamps.

Nate takes the decoy box and begins his descent. He can just reach the corners of the box to hold it with his arms completely extended. Leaning backwards, he can't really see where he's stepping. Roller skate? Maybe better to back down the stairs and rest the box on successive stairs. Turning around in the stairwell isn't easy, but the box seems somehow smaller, easier to hold, but heavier. He sets it on the stair above him waist level, halfway down to the landing where there isn't a room with lamps. Looking down. The door is shut now. Did he shut it? Now the box feels like it's completely filled with books. She must have added to the duckies. Below the landing he's holding it in a bear hug – it's definitely smaller, and by the time he's down in the kitchen, it's down to the size of a case of wine. He's carried them in from his father's car. Wine by the case, his father says, will have to do until the tanker trucks can be persuaded to make deliveries.

Mrs. Price must still be in the tower room. More piano music. This time Chopin. That E Minor Prelude straining to make E flat. Old pitch. For that, you'd need an old pitch fork. Look in the box which once was another box, slight of his own hand? Of course.

Now back up the stairs to find the old lady and collect the five spot. She'll meet him halfway, at the landing. But first the Scarbo from Ravel's Gaspard de la Nuit.

Ghostly fingers in the turret, tapping keyboards. Some of the pianos produce pitches, hammers striking strings. Others slap and moan. Doorknobs settle. Ask for your favorites, dear reader. There's time.

"This is the room I meant," Nate points to the door, "where I found the door knob and my glove. And the door was open."

The old lady is ashen. Her wen might sprout wings and fly away.

"This is the closed room. It can't be entered."

Nate realizes she's always been ashen. She flutters her hand at him, at the door, deprecating or dusting, Nate can't tell.

"It's not closed off," he says, feeling a second wind of stubbornness buoying him.

He turns the knob and the door opens, not easily – he has to push it a bit, but it's an old house, and doors in old houses...

The old lady might as well be singing, *la la la* – he's tuned her out – she's nattering about his $5. About heating old houses and doors nailed shut. It's the same room, Nate's happy to see, but not in the same mood. The lamps aren't lit and the window at the far end is giving the only light. It's not curtained anymore. None of the lamps on the tables are lit. The knickknacks and china gargoyles and every solid object pretend to be covered by, are hiding under layers of... calcium carbonate, volcanic ash, eider down, cottonwood fluff... No, it's just dust. Just dust. Unjust dust. That old woman and her *la la la*. Nate's not going to stop until he gets to the window and the table with a candle – no candle now, and the string quartet alcove is more like a hallway. At the end of it, too far to make out, he saw this in the box, after he took out the books, the decoys, all tangled together, the eggs, round stones, an old scythe, his guitar transported here from the front porch across the street, fishing lures, a little photo album, pictures of a dog, and a photo of a bridge, odd angle, looking up...

The hallway ends in a dirt road and Nate's not in that house, nor is he exactly standing in the road but it's not the less clear to him. The father's pulling up the son who's all dripping, miserable, having hurt his leg and fallen into the creek. Nate's father showed him the scar. After all those years, smooth and hairless, approximately the shape of Lake Michigan. Before that, the moment when his father is fishing and something heaved and shouldered: it's a really big fish now, a Sasquatch of a fish, and there's a snake, too – a snake that flairs up like a flushed grouse. There's always a snake in a story like this. Nate can put their stories together, place them in the car and send them home. It's a long way home. And this might be the time they run out of gas. The time they run out of gas and see the fireflies. Ten thousand fireflies. They come in jars. Filled by the fathers and their fathers. Why not?

Fathers give sons the story, and then it's theirs to tell.